ACADEMY OF DANCE

written by
Margaret Gurevich

cover illustration by Claire Almon
interior illustrations by Addy Rivera Sonda

STONE ARCH BOOKS
a capstone imprint

Academy of Dance is published by Stone Arch Books
A Capstone Imprint
1710 Roe Crest Drive
North Mankato, Minnesota 56003
www.mycapstone.com

Library of Congress Cataloging-in-Publication Data
Names: Gurevich, Margaret, author. | Sonda, Addy Rivera, illustrator.
Title: On pointe / by Margaret Gurevich ; illustrated by Addy Rivera Sonda.
Description: North Mankato, Minnesota : Stone Arch Books, [2019] | Series: Academy of Dance | Summary: After years of ballet Jada feels she is ready to go "on pointe," but the whole process is a lot more complicated than she ever realized: from being measured and fitted for the shoes to tying the laces correctly, she still has a lot to learn, and that is before she actually tries to walk in pointe shoes, which seems to use muscles she was barely aware of—for the first time Jada finds that ballet hurts.
Identifiers: LCCN 2018037073| ISBN 9781496578228 (hardcover) | ISBN 9781496580207 (pbk.) | ISBN 9781496578242 (ebook pdf)
Subjects: LCSH: Dance schools—Juvenile fiction. | Ballet—Equipment and supplies—Juvenile fiction. | Self-confidence—Juvenile fiction. | Best friends—Juvenile fiction. | CYAC: Ballet dancing—Fiction. | Shoes—Fiction. | Self-confidence—Fiction. | Best friends—Fiction. | Friendship—Fiction.
Classification: LCC PZ7.G98146 On 2019 | DDC 813.6 [Fic]—dc23
LC record available at https://lccn.loc.gov/2018037073

Designer: Kayla Rossow

Printed and bound in China.
966

TABLE OF CONTENTS

CHAPTER 1

Ready for More

I rise on the balls of my feet for the *relevé,* curve my arms in front so my fingertips touch, and twirl across the smooth hardwood. Each time my toes glide across the studio floors at Ms. Marianne's Academy of Dance it feels like magic.

Ms. Marianne herself paces the floor and monitors our footing, balance, and form. Her salt-and-pepper hair is pulled back into its usual bun, and her burgundy scarf matches her leotard.

I bend my knees for a *plié* and smile as the rest of the girls do the same. It's hard to believe I was once nervous about coming here.

My family and I moved from Philadelphia to New Jersey less than a year ago. I didn't want to leave the noises of the city, my friends, my old dance team, or my old dance school.

At first I thought I would never fit in. But then I found Ms. Marianne's. After a rocky start, I met amazing girls on the dance team who became my best friends. Now Ms. Marianne's feels like a second home.

I rise on my tiptoes again and perform a *soutenu* turn, keeping my arms curved in front of me.

"Beautiful form, Jada!" Ms. Marianne calls.

I smile in response, keeping my focus on my dancing. Grace Jenkins, one of my best friends, grins and silently claps her hands. Grace is a tap dancer, but everyone at Ms. Marianne's is required to take Wednesday's all-team ballet class.

"*Chassé*, ladies!" Ms. Marianne says above the music.

I line up beside my two other best friends, Gabby Sanchez and Brie Benson. Even though ballet is supposed to be serious, it's hard to keep a straight face when the four of us get together. Ms. Marianne gives us a warning look, but I can tell she's trying to keep from smiling.

As the music speeds up, my feet glide across the floor, faster and faster.

"*Piqué* turns!" calls Ms. Marianne.

Piqué turns are a beginner move, and I've been doing ballet for years, so it's easy to want to breeze through them. But I've learned to be patient and take my time. I keep my arms open wide in second position and move my right foot forward, careful to keep it straight and pointed. My left toe meets my right knee as I turn and close my arms in front of me.

"And one and two and three," Ms. Marianne calls as all the dancers do three *piqué* turns in a row. I spot the corner beside the window each time I turn to keep my balance.

We end the class with one of my favorite jumps, the *changement*. I place my feet in fifth position with my right leg in front, toes touching the heels. Then I jump up and land in fifth position, this time with my left leg in front.

When class ends, I notice Ms. Marianne studying me. I want to find out why, but before I can approach, another dancer starts talking to her. I decide whatever it is can wait. There's somewhere I want to be.

"Come on!" I say to Gabby, Brie, and Grace. "Let's go before we miss it."

I lead the way, and in seconds we're standing outside the pointe dance class. We push our faces close to the glass and watch the ballerinas.

My friends all focus on different forms of dance—tap, jazz, and hip-hop. But that doesn't stop them from appreciating how challenging pointe is.

Brie lets out a low whistle. "I don't think I could ever trade in my hip-hop sneakers for those shoes."

"Right?" says Gabby, brushing her dark hair from her eyes. "There are a lot of ballet moves in jazz, but I can't even imagine standing on my toes like that!"

Grace's curly blonde hair sneaks out of its bun as she nods. "Jada can do it." She winks and puts her arm around me.

The ballerinas' strong calf muscles stand out as they *plié*. I run my hand along my own calves. I know they're strong.

"You really think so?" I ask my friends hopefully.

"For sure!" says Gabby, bumping me with her hip. "I noticed Ms. Marianne paying extra attention to your movements today. I bet that's why."

"Yes!" Brie says a little too loudly and blushes. "You should totally talk to her! You'd be amazing at pointe!"

I look at the pointe dancers one more time. Then I close my eyes and picture myself beside them, pointe shoes on, moving gracefully across the floor. Maybe my friends are right. Maybe I'm ready for more.

CHAPTER 2

Pointe Potential

During ballet practice the next day, I can barely focus. All I can think about is talking to Ms. Marianne about pointe. I spent the past twenty-four hours practicing the speech in my head, and I'm ready. As soon as class ends, I rush across the floor and skid to a stop beside Ms. Marianne.

"Jada!" Ms. Marianne takes a step back to avoid bumping into me.

"S-sorry," I stutter. I clear my throat and try to remember the speech I planned.

"What can I do for you?" my instructor asks kindly.

Just spit it out, I tell myself. "I want to take pointe," I say.

Ms. Marianne raises an eyebrow and places her index finger on her chin. But she doesn't say anything.

Nervously I continue. "My calves and ankles are strong. I think I'm ready." I remember what my friends told me yesterday and hope I sound confident. "I know I'm ready."

Ms. Marianne laces her fingers together and nods. "I think you're ready too. I've been studying you the past few weeks in class. Your posture and balance have been impressive. You've always been a great dancer, but you've grown even stronger."

I bite my tongue so I don't squeal out loud. If Ms. Marianne were Gabby, Brie, or Grace, I would grab her hands and jump up and down, but Ms. Marianne is too calm for that.

"Thank you!" I exclaim. "I'm so glad to hear you say that. So what's next?"

Ms. Marianne laughs. "Pointe is very exciting, but it is a process. First we need to find the right shoes. After that you need to break them in. And after *that* . . ."

After that I zone out. I see Ms. Marianne's lips moving, but I can't focus on her words. All I can think about is starting pointe! Besides, I've been dancing for more than seven years. I know I can handle whatever is thrown at me.

"Jada?" Ms. Marianne says, bringing me back to planet Earth. She looks worried, but I'm not sure why.

"I've got this," I reassure her. "I can do it."

Ms. Marianne nods slowly. "I'm glad you're confident. I just want you to remember that it takes *time* to feel comfortable in the shoes. They *will* hurt."

"I can handle it," I say confidently.

"Just remember that pointe affects some students' feet more than others. Even students like you, who appear physically ready, may not be mentally ready for the toll the shoes can take."

I don't understand how someone can *seem* ready but not be. Ms. Marianne said I was strong and had good balance.

What more do you need? I think. Still, I nod to show I'm listening.

"You are a wonderful dancer," she goes on, "but if—at any time—you decide pointe isn't for you, please speak up. It's not for everyone, and that's *fine*."

This must be the speech she gives to everyone. I want to roll my eyes, but I know that would be rude. "I never step away from a challenge," I say, grinning at her.

Ms. Marianne looks as if she wants to say something else but changes her mind. "Very well," she says. "I'll call your mother, and we'll arrange a time for the three of us to go shopping for pointe shoes. Remember to wear tights."

"Thank you!" I gush. When a sentence has my two favorite words—*pointe* and *shopping*—what could be better?

CHAPTER 3

SHOE SHOPPING

"Come on!" I call over my shoulder to Mom as I run down the sidewalk on Saturday.

"I'm trying, but some of us aren't speedy teenagers!" Mom calls as she jogs to match my pace.

Normally when my mom and I go shopping for ballet stuff, I stand in front of the window first and check out the display. But today there's no time to wait.

I head into the store immediately. Inside the shelves are full of everything from leotards to shoes to duffel bags with ballerinas embroidered on them.

I look past all the equipment, my eyes scanning the store for Ms. Marianne. She waves to me from the pointe section, and I sprint to join her.

"She's very excited," my mom says as she joins us. She puts her arm around me.

Ms. Marianne smiles warmly. "It's a very big deal. I still remember when I got *my* first pair of pointe shoes. I was thirteen, just like Jada."

Let's just start! I want to shout.

A short, older lady walks up to us. "I'm Doreen, and I'll be your fitter today," she says.

"Fitter?" I ask, confused. "When I bought ballet shoes, I just tried on my shoe size."

"Not with pointe shoes, my dear," says Doreen. "We need to measure the width of your foot, arch height, and length of your toe. The shape of your foot also matters. Have a seat, please."

Doreen motions to the seat as if she's inviting a queen to sit on a throne, and I giggle. Once I'm seated she moves my feet back and forth. Then she asks me to stand and sit so she can see my feet at different angles. She scribbles notes onto a small, yellow pad.

When she's done—more than twenty minutes later—Doreen disappears behind a curtain at the back of the store to look for shoes that best match my feet. Soon she's back with a cart piled high with boxes. All the top pointe shoe brands are there.

"I can't believe these are all for me!" I exclaim as I grab one of the boxes and toss the lid off.

"Put these on your toes first," says Doreen handing me something soft that looks like toe mittens. "They'll make dancing in your pointe shoes less painful."

I put the mittens on. Then I shove my foot into the shoe and . . . stop. Something's wrong.

"They're all going to be uncomfortable at first," Ms. Marianne says, reading my face.

"That's why I have a list of what to look for," says Doreen, flipping a page in her notepad.

My shoulders slump a little. Apparently when Ms. Marianne said, "It is a process," she didn't just mean dancing.

"Since your feet are a little wide," says Doreen, "I chose shoes with a square box." She points to the top of the shoe. "I also think a shorter vamp—the length of the box—is best so that you can get fully up on pointe. There's also the shank, the part that supports the arch. Your teacher and I like a softer shank so the shoes can be broken in more easily. It will help strengthen your arches, which is very important so you don't hurt yourself."

I nod slowly. Getting pointe shoes is not going to be simple.

"Can you wiggle your toes?" Ms. Marianne asks.

"Yes!" I say happily.

"Then they're the wrong fit," says Doreen. "They should fit like a glove. No wiggle room."

"Oh." I take off the shoes and try on another pair. "Definitely no wiggle room here. My toes are on top of each other."

"Off," says Doreen. "Your toes shouldn't be squished together either."

I sigh and try on another pair. And another. And another. More than an hour later, I *finally* have my shoes.

"Thanks so much," my mom says to Doreen. "This was quite the experience!"

"Now I can go home and dance!" I say, my excitement returning.

Doreen and Ms. Marianne exchange looks.

"What?" I say. I can hear the whine in my voice.

"You need to sew on the ribbons first, then learn how to tie them. Even then, I don't want you trying any ballet moves without me," says Ms. Marianne firmly. "I mentioned that when we talked the other day."

I feel my face get hot. That must have been the part I wasn't really listening to.

I put the shoes back into their box and lace up my sneakers. Ms. Marianne and Doreen tell my mom how to sew the ribbons onto my shoes. Then they tell us how to lace the shoes. I try to pay attention, but it's hard. All I can think is that it will be *forever* before I actually get to dance in my new pointe shoes.

"Congratulations!" Ms. Marianne says as we exit the store. "Why don't you come by the studio tomorrow morning? We'll start breaking them in."

"Tomorrow? Really?" I say, feeling relieved. "I'll be there!"

Maybe forever isn't as far away as I thought.

CHAPTER 4

Pointe Ready

"I'm pointe ready!" I say as I run into the studio the next morning.

Ms. Marianne laughs. "I'm still waiting for my coffee to kick in."

"I'm so hyped up, I don't need caffeine." I take my pointe shoes out of the box and slip them on. My mom sewed the ribbons on last night, and I proudly tie the ribbons in a bow.

"Very nice," Ms. Marianne says. "I just have a few minor adjustments. First of all, never tie the ribbons in a bow. Bows can come undone. You should double knot them, just between your ankle bone and your Achilles tendon."

"Oh, OK," I say, nodding.

"Then you tuck in the knot and the loose ends of the ribbons," she continues. "We don't want to see the knot. Here, I'll show you."

Ms. Marianne laces the ribbons around my ankle. I watch carefully. Then she undoes her work and hands the ribbons to me so I can practice tying them. It takes four tries to get them perfect.

"See how the ribbons cross in the middle of your ankle?" Ms. Marianne points out. I nod. "That's how you know you tied them correctly," she explains. "Ribbons help support your ankles, so we can't cut corners and risk injury."

Just like when we were shopping for shoes, I'm eager to get started. But one look at Ms. Marianne's serious face tells me all these little details are just as important as dancing.

"I understand," I say.

"Good," says Ms. Marianne. "I need you to be patient. Because as I said the other day, it's—"

I grin. "A process."

"That's right." Ms. Marianne winks at me. "Before you walk on the shoes, we need to crush the box. Softening the front of the shoe will make it fit better around your toe joints."

"Oh!" I say excitedly. "I saw that on YouTube. Dancers slam the front of the shoe inside a door."

Ms. Marianne looks horrified. "We are *not* doing that," she says firmly. "Too many things could go wrong, like crushing your finger. Step on it with your heel instead."

The door idea seemed more fun, but I do as Ms. Marianne says. I untie the ribbons, slip my shoes off, and place them on the ground. Then I use my heels to soften each shoe's toe box.

"There you go," says Ms. Marianne. "Now hold the canvas of each shoe with both hands and pull it up so it bends. It's called bending the shank. It will help with the fit. Be careful not to snap the shank in half."

I follow Ms. Marianne's instructions, treating my shoes like glass. They're so special, I don't want to ruin them. When I'm done, I look at her. I know these steps are important, but I'm ready to dance!

Ms. Marianne's eyes twinkle. "You think you're ready to begin now?"

"Yes!" I exclaim.

"Fabulous," says Ms. Marianne. "To start breaking them in, I want you to walk across the floor and back in *demi pointe*. That's just walking on the balls of your feet, not on your toes."

"Got it," I say. It may be only *demi pointe*, but at least I'll get to do something in my new shoes!

I put my shoes back on and tie the ribbons, just like Ms. Marianne showed me. Then I rise onto the balls of my feet and take my first steps.

Almost immediately I feel a pull on my calves. There's a tightening in my toes too. I keep going until I reach the mirror. Then I turn around and walk back to Ms. Marianne.

"How do the shoes feel?" she asks.

I shrug and keep walking. The truth is they hurt, but I don't want to admit that. Not when I'm finally getting to use them.

"You looked good out there," says Ms. Marianne. "Can you try that one more time?"

I want to say I'd like a break, but we've barely done anything. A serious dancer would push through, wouldn't she?

"Sure," I say. I rise onto the balls of my feet again and start walking.

"Let's do a few *relevés* and grand *pliés* at the barre," chirps Ms. Marianne.

"Sounds good," I say brightly, trying to match Ms. Marianne's cheery tone.

I must not sound entirely convincing, because Ms. Marianne studies my face. "Jada, it's normal for your feet to be uncomfortable. If you aren't up for more today, it's *completely* fine. You're a beginner."

I bristle. I haven't thought of myself as a *beginner* since I was five years old. I take a deep breath and let it out.

"Thank you," I say, putting a fake smile on my face, "but I can do it."

I place my hand on the barre, bend my knees, and lift my heels as I come up for the *grand plié*.

"Again," says Ms. Marianne. "To dance *en pointe*, it's very important you get used to the motions and break in the shoes."

I nod. I finish the *grand pliés* and practice rising to high *demi pointe* for the *relevés.*

"Up," says Ms. Marianne, "and down. And up. And down."

I sigh. Not only are the shoes uncomfortable, but the moves are boring. I feel as if I'm five all over again.

Finally Ms. Marianne claps. "OK, I think that's enough for today. You're off to a great start! Practice these moves at home, and I'll see you at the beginner pointe class on Tuesday."

"Then I'll finally be able to stand on my toes?" I ask.

Ms. Marianne nods. "Yes. I know it's hard, but be patient. It may have been hundreds of years ago," she teases, "but I remember how you feel."

This time when I smile, it's real. "Thank you." I don't know if Ms. Marianne really knows how I feel, but it's still nice of her to say it.

CHAPTER 5

BEGINNER BLUES

Can't wait to hear about your first pointe class!!!

I grin when the message from Brie pops up on the group text I have with her, Grace, and Gabby on Monday afternoon. My friends' support always gives me confidence.

Today's class will be great! I tell myself. Sunday was about breaking in my shoes, but today I'll actually get to go on my toes.

I'm already in the studio, waiting for class to start. Everyone around me is lacing up their ribbons. I do the same, then grab an open space at the barre to practice my *pliés* and *demi pointes.*

Finally I rise to my toes. I feel the difference immediately and go back down. I stretch my ankles and try again. My ankles and toes hurt, but I shake it off.

It's a process, I tell myself, echoing Ms. Marianne.

A moment later, Ms. Marianne herself walks in. She claps her hands to signal the start of class. "Places, ladies! We will begin with the *sous-sus.*"

That's such a beginner move! I think. *I've got this!*

I place my feet in fifth position, my toes and heels touching, and sink down into a *plié.* Then I spring back up onto the tips of my toes.

"Ouch," I mutter as I stumble.

I do the same move again—slower this time—and get it. Kind of. I watch the other dancers match Ms. Marianne's rhythm.

Every other girl makes the rise from *plié* to *sous-sus* look easy. A *sous-sus* is a move I've done countless times. It *should* be easy.

You've never done it in pointe shoes! a voice in my head taunts.

"*Plié, sous-sus.* Again!" calls Ms. Marianne as she walks around.

I sink down and try to spring back up, but I stumble. No one else does. No one else looks like she's in pain. I do the moves again and wince.

"Two feet!" Ms. Marianne calls.

We *plié* and quickly rise to our toes while holding onto the barre.

"Two feet! One foot! Two feet! One foot!" Ms. Marianne sings as she walks around the room.

I grit my teeth as I *plié* and rise to two toes, then one, two, then one. My calves and ankles are killing me. I feel my toes scrape painfully against the insides of my pointe shoes.

Is the skin scraping off? Are they bruised and bloody? Is it supposed to be this painful? I try not to think about it.

"How are you, Jada?" Ms. Marianne asks as she walks behind me.

I force a smile, but don't say anything. I don't want her to think I can't handle it.

Ms. Marianne pats my shoulder. "You're doing a great job, but to be on the safe side, why don't you switch into your ballet shoes after the next exercise? I don't want you to overdo it on the first day."

I want to protest—I should be able to keep up with the other dancers. I'm not some beginner. But before I can say anything, Ms. Marianne is already moving away.

"Let's step away from the barre now," Ms. Marianne instructs. "Keep moving through your warm-ups."

I gingerly let go of the barre. Doing these exercises with the barre for support was hard enough. Without the barre it will be torture.

Don't think about the pain. You can do it. I keep repeating the phrases in my head as I *plié,* then spring to my toes, but they're not helping.

Suddenly Ms. Marianne is beside me again. "I think it's best to stop now," she says quietly.

No matter how much I fake it, I can't trick her. I walk to the side, take off my shoes, and slip on my ballet slippers. Even though my toes, ankles, and calves are sore, my ballet slippers feel like clouds.

I watch the rest of the dancers finish their warm-up, then twirl on their toes. They look so amazing.

My heart sinks. *Were they ever in my very painful shoes?* I wonder. *Will I ever look like them?*

CHAPTER 6

A Big Adjustment

"What happened?" Grace asks the next day, staring at my bandaged feet. We're all gathered in the studio to warm up before our all-team ballet class.

When I took off my tights after pointe class last night, my toes were bleeding. Blisters were forming on my heels and the sides of my feet. This morning, my feet were still a mess.

I readjust the bandages and carefully pull my tights on over the top. "Pointe class happened," I reply.

Brie frowns. "Sorry," she says. "That looks painful."

I shrug as if it doesn't bother me. Except it does. "I looked it up online, and all the ballet sites say it's common to get blisters when you first start pointe," I say.

"Maybe you should talk to Ms. Marianne," Gabby suggests.

I shake my head. "I don't want her to say I can't do it."

Brie bites her lip. "Are you sure?"

I slip on my ballet slippers and *plié,* trying not to grimace. "See? No problem."

My friends exchange a worried look, but before they can say anything else, Ms. Marianne enters the studio. Everyone moves to the barre for warm-ups.

Plié and up. *Plié* and up. I straighten my back to keep smooth lines in my torso.

"Lovely form, ladies," says Ms. Marianne. "Now *relevé*!"

I rise to my tiptoes, and my ankles hurt. I bite my lip to stop myself from crying out as I slowly lower my feet to the floor.

"*Relevé, arabesque,*" Ms. Marianne calls as she walks across the floor.

And up, I tell myself as I rise to the balls of my feet again. I lift my leg behind me for the *arabesque* and try to block out the pain in my ankles.

Each time Ms. Marianne looks in my direction, I work on keeping my face emotionless. If she sees I'm in pain, she'll think I can't handle pointe.

"Line up for grand *jetés,*" Ms. Marianne instructs.

My stomach drops. If I'm feeling pain with simple moves like *pliés* and *relevés,* the jumps will be agony.

You can do this, I tell myself. If only pep talks were enough.

When it's my turn to leap across the floor, I close my eyes and hope for the best. My feet leave the ground, and I do the splits in the air.

Thud.

All too soon, I land on the hard, wooden floor. This time I can't stop from crying out.

Ms. Marianne comes up behind me. "I think you should sit out the rest of the class," she says. "Your feet need to recover."

Tears spring to my eyes. I can't keep up in pointe, and now I'm being forced to sit out ballet too?

"I'm fine," I insist. "I can shake it off."

Ms. Marianne puts her hand on my arm. "Jada, your safety is the most important thing," she says firmly. "Have a seat."

I grit my teeth to stop myself from crying in front of everyone. Then I grab my water bottle and walk out of the class.

Through the large window beside the door I watch everyone else *jeté, pirouette,* and *chassé* across the floor. My friends smile in between jumps, twirls, and glides.

I wanted a challenge, but this is not what I imagined. I expected pointe to be hard, but I never thought my ballet would suffer too.

CHAPTER 7

A Lot Like Quitting

I read online that calluses form on your toes the longer you do pointe, so instead of resting my feet that night, I decide to practice the moves from my first pointe class. It's painful, but I know I'm ready for pointe. I must be.

The next morning, I realize that pushing through the pain might have been a *bad* decision. My feet are in even worse shape than yesterday.

I change the bloody Band-Aids and wrap Ace bandages around my sore ankles. Each time my heels graze the back of my sneakers, I feel the blisters scrape. But I'm determined not to let that stop me.

Jada
BANDAGES

My soft ballet slippers will feel better, I tell myself as I head to the studio for my ballet class. I get there thirty minutes early. Ms. Marianne is already there.

"How are you feeling today?" she asks when I walk in.

"Hanging in," I say with a brave smile.

Ms. Marianne looks concerned. "Jada, I'd like to talk to you for a minute," she says. "Remember when I said you reminded me of myself?"

I nod. "I won't disappoint you."

"That's not what I meant," she says gently. "You're a wonderful dancer, and I know how eager you were to start pointe. I was eager too. My ankles were strong, and I was great at my jumps. I was sure I was ready."

I can see where this conversation is going. I frown. "I *am* ready."

Ms. Marianne smiles sympathetically. "I let you try pointe because your ankles *are* strong. But even the best dancers progress at different stages. Starting earlier or later doesn't make someone better. I started at your age, but it turned out I wasn't ready. It was painful, and I *hated* that it stopped me from dancing in my regular ballet classes."

I'm surprised. "What did you do?"

"I took a break until I was more prepared. When I started pointe again at sixteen, my ankles and feet were stronger. I was mentally ready, and I knew what to expect. It was much easier." She looks at me and raises one eyebrow.

I look down at the floor. I know Ms. Marianne wants me to make the same decision she did. A part of me wants that too. But another part of me feels as if stopping now is the same thing as giving up.

"Think about it," says Ms. Marianne.

I raise my head to look at Ms. Marianne's kind eyes. "I will."

"There's something else," she continues. "I noticed you limping before—"

I cut her off. "I'm fine now."

"Jada," Ms. Marianne says firmly, "it's my responsibility to make sure my students are safe. Before class starts, I'd like you to show me some basic moves and jumps. If you can do them, I'll back off. If not, I'm afraid you'll have to sit out today's class."

"What would you like me to do?" I ask quietly, walking to the barre by the mirrors.

"Let's start with *plié* to *relevé*," says Ms. Marianne.

I bend my knees as I lower myself toward the floor. Then I slowly straighten my legs as I rise to the balls of my feet.

The whole time I wonder if my teacher is as frustrated with me as I am with myself.

After a moment, Ms. Marianne turns on the music. I try to keep up with it, but my ankles throb, making it impossible.

Ms. Marianne frowns. "That's all I need to see. I'm not going to torture you with *chassés* and *jetés*."

"Do you want me to stay and watch the others?" I ask. That's what I had to do when I sprained my ankle last year. Ms. Marianne thinks it's important for dancers to support their teammates and keep the routine fresh in their minds, even if they can't dance.

Ms. Marianne studies my face and shakes her head. "Not if you don't want to. But promise me two things. One, stay off the pointe shoes. You can't heal if you keep pushing yourself."

I hang my head.

"Two, think about what I said before. It's not quitting. Just . . . waiting."

I feel a tear slipping down my cheek. It sounds a lot like quitting to *me*. Still, I mumble what Ms. Marianne wants to hear. "I promise."

CHAPTER 8

Decision Time

"You have another pointe class tomorrow, right?" asks Grace on Saturday night. She, Gabby, Brie, and I are all sitting in Gabby's basement snacking on the crispy plantains her *abuela* made. We're all spending the night here tonight.

"That's the plan," I say, crunching down on a plantain.

"Are your feet better?" Brie asks, reaching across me for another plantain.

"Finally," I say.

"But?" Grace says. She always seems to be able to read my mind.

I haven't told my friends about my conversation with Ms. Marianne. I've been a little afraid they'll agree with her. Or maybe I've been afraid they *won't.* I wring my hands.

"Ms. Marianne and I talked on Thursday. . . ." I say. "She thinks I should stop pointe. For now, at least."

"Did she say why?" Gabby asks. "Because your feet have been hurting?"

"That's a big part of it," I say. "But she also thinks it's taking me away from ballet, and I'm struggling to do both."

"What do *you* think?" asks Grace.

I'm so confused I don't know where to start. "I really want to do pointe. I was so sure I was ready for it," I say, trying to weed through all the thoughts in my head.

Brie furrows her brow. "And now you think you're not?"

I throw my hands up, frustrated. "I don't know! I don't know what to think. My feet were bleeding for days. My ankles hurt so much, I couldn't barely do a basic *plié*." I wince, remembering the pain.

"Wow," says Gabby. "I knew your feet were bothering you, but I didn't realize they were that bad!"

I blush. "I didn't want anyone to think I couldn't handle pointe." I pause. "I was trying to convince *myself* I was fine."

Gabby chews the inside of her cheek, deep in thought. "Did Ms. Marianne have any advice?"

I sigh. "Just that I should take a break and try again when I'm older."

Brie looks thoughtful. "This isn't exactly the same, but remember when Gabby and I both went out for the solo last year?"

"Unfortunately," I say, wrinkling my nose. The whole experience almost ruined their friendship.

Brie makes a face too and laughs. "Yeah, not an experience I want to repeat. But the *good* part about it was that the solo went to a more experienced dancer. It taught us that if we keep practicing, we'll get there one day too."

"Right," adds Gabby. "There's more to learn. We don't have to do it all right now."

"And Ms. Marianne is always adding new classes," Grace adds. "You never know what might pop up."

I get up and pace around Gabby's basement. My friends make good points, but I know what's really bothering me. "But isn't it quitting?" I ask softly.

"No way," says Grace. "Our best friend is not a quitter. Think of all you've accomplished."

"New state, new dance team, new friends," Gabby says, counting on her fingers.

"Even last year when you hurt your ankle—" Brie starts.

"Oh, you mean when I felt sorry for myself?" I interrupt.

Brie waves her hand. "Maybe a little, but then you pushed yourself to practice and get better. You did amazing at our first competition."

Grace jumps off the couch and puts her arm around me. "You know you'll go back to pointe." She pauses. "Right?"

I think about what my friends are saying. Then I consider what will happen if I stay with pointe now. Chances are it won't be any different than last week. My ankles will throb. My toes will bleed. It'll be back to Ace bandages and Band-Aids. The thought of hobbling around, not being able to even do ballet, is unbearable.

Grace nudges me. "Jada?"

A part of me still hates the idea of stopping something I've started, but Grace is right. I can use this time to keep getting better at ballet. Keep doing what I love. And when I'm ready, follow my pointe dream too.

"Of course I'll go back to it," I say.

"Then that's your answer," says Gabby.

CHAPTER 9

Not Giving Up

The next morning, my stomach is a jumble of nerves. I know Ms. Marianne will agree with my decision, but I'm still a little nervous to tell her.

"Jada!" Ms. Marianne says when I walk into the studio the next morning. "You're here early."

I make my way over and take a deep breath. I don't know why getting the words out is so hard. "I thought about what you said the other day," I start. "You were right. I'll try pointe again when I'm a little older."

I know I'm making the right decision. I also know Ms. Marianne thinks this is the right decision, and *she's* the expert.

It was the idea of giving up that was holding me back, I realized. There was a knot in my stomach, scaring me into thinking that this was my one chance to advance. But after talking with my friends and really thinking it through, I realized I would never let myself give up on my dreams.

"Oh, honey," Ms. Marianne says, giving me a hug. "I know it's hard, but it's very important you don't see this as a forever decision. It's just—"

"Waiting," I say quietly.

"That's right. You're a talented dancer, and I don't want you to miss out on doing what you love. It's OK to wait until you're ready. And"—she pauses—"this is not giving up."

I nod. It's still hard not to feel sad. I don't want to run away from things. I only want to run *toward* something.

"I want to hear you say it," Ms. Marianne says. "Come on, humor me. 'This is not giving up.'"

"This is not giving up," I repeat, feeling silly.

"Again," says Ms. Marianne.

"This is not giving up," I say.

Even though I finally believe these words, hearing them out loud makes me feel even better about my decision. I smile. "Thank you."

"I should be thanking *you,*" Ms. Marianne replies. "You inspired me to start a new class."

My eyes widen. "*I* did?"

"You brought back all the feelings I had when I had to stop pointe. It made me think that maybe there's a better way," says Ms. Marianne. "Beginning next week, I'm starting a weekly pre-pointe class. We'll strengthen your ankles and learn new dancing techniques. The goal will be to get dancers' feet pointe ready *before* they start wearing pointe shoes."

"That sounds amazing!" I exclaim. It's just like Grace said: *You never know what might pop up!*

"I know you want a challenge and a chance to learn something new," continues Ms. Marianne. "This is a way to do that, minus the pain and stress. When you're ready to try pointe again, you'll be that much closer to success."

My stomach is jumpy again, but this time it's from excitement. I walked into Ms. Marianne's a bundle of nerves, but I'm leaving filled with new possibilities.

ABOUT THE AUTHOR

Margaret Gurevich is the author of many books for kids, including Capstone's *Gina's Balance, Aerials and Envy,* and the award-winning Chloe by Design series. She has also written for *National Geographic Kids* and Penguin Young Readers. While Margaret hasn't done performance dance since she was a tween, this series has inspired her to take dance classes again. She lives in New Jersey with her son and husband.

ABOUT THE ILLUSTRATOR

Addy Rivera Sonda is a Mexican illustrator currently living in Los Angeles, California. She loves color and nature. They inspire her to think that stories and art are slowly but surely changing the way people understand themselves and perceive others, building empathy and a more inclusive world.

GLOSSARY

accomplish (uh-KOM-plish)—to do something successfully

Achilles tendon (uh-KIL-eez TEN-duhn)—the body part that connects the muscles of the lower leg to the heel's bone

barre (bahr)—the horizontal wooden bar used by dancers for support and balance

bristle (BRIS-uhl)—to show signs of anger

plantain (PLAN-tayn)—the greenish fruit of a kind of banana plant that is eaten cooked and is larger, less sweet, and more starchy than the ordinary banana

posture (POS-cher)—the position of your body

rhythm (RITH-uhm)—a regular, repeated pattern of beats, sounds, activity, or movements

unbearable (uhn-BAIR-uh-buhl)—something so bad or unpleasant that you cannot stand it

TALK ABOUT IT!

1. Jada is excited to start learning pointe, but Ms. Marianne tells her she might not be ready. Talk about a time you felt ready to learn something in school or in a club, but were told you weren't ready.

2. When Jada begins practicing point, she doesn't tell Ms. Marianne or her friends how much pain she's in. Talk about why you think she stays quiet.

3. Jada is worried people will think she's a quitter if she waits to continue learning pointe. Why do you think she feels this way?

WRITE ABOUT IT!

1. Jada and her friends each belong to a different dance group, practicing ballet, tap dance, jazz, and hip-hop. Write about which dance group you would join if you went to Ms. Marianne's Academy of Dance.

2. Starting pointe lessons gives Jada some problems. Write down some of the dangers of starting pointe.

3. Jada begins pointe before she's really ready for it. Write down some reasons she'll be more prepared to start pointe the next time she tries.

MORE ABOUT POINTE

When you think about ballet, what do you picture? Graceful ballerinas balanced on the tips of their toes? If that's the case, you're actually thinking about pointe. Pointe is a technique—and part of ballet—in which a dancer supports all of her body weight on the tips of her toes while wearing special shoes called pointe shoes.

So what does it take to be pointe ready? There are several factors to think about, including a dancer's strength, age, technique, and experience:

- Typically a dancer should have at least 2–4 years of ballet experience before attempting pointe work.

- Most dancers don't start learning pointe until 12–14 years old. Before that, the bones of the foot aren't fully developed. Permanent foot injuries could occur as a result of starting pointe too early.

- In addition to strong feet, pointe dancers must have strong ankles and legs. These are crucial for a dancer to be able to stay on pointe for the length of a routine. A strong core helps with balance and is essential to ensure a dancer doesn't roll her feet while dancing.

- During the first year of pointe, dancers can expect to take 3–4 ballet classes per week.

MORE ABOUT POINTE

Want to learn more? Here are a few moves all ballet dancers should know:

arabesque—a ballet move where the dancer stands on one leg and extends the other behind

chassé—a ballet move where the dancer makes quick, gliding steps

jeté—a move in ballet where the dancer extends one leg then jumps with the other

pirouette—a full turn on the front of one foot in ballet

plié—a move where a dancer stands with his or her feet turned out, then bends and straightens the knees

relevé—a ballet move where a dancer looks as if he or she is standing on his or her toes

sous-sus—a ballet move that means "over-under" and describes when a dancer quickly rises from *demi-plié* onto pointe, placing the back foot closely behind the front in fifth position with fully stretched legs

soutenu—a turn in ballet where the dancer turns in *sous-sus* or fifth position *en pointe* and ends with the opposite foot in front

COOK-OFF AMERICA

Food Photography: Alec Fatalevich
Location Photography: Alec Fatalevich
Editing: Barbara King
Research: Deanna Sison

ISBN 0-9705973-3-9

Printed in Korea

10 9 8 7 6 5 4 3 2 1

Marjorie Poore Productions
363 14th Avenue
San Francisco, CA 94118

COOK-OFF AMERICA
Produced by Marjorie Poore Productions
Photography by Alec Fatalevich
MORE PRIZE-WINNING RECIPES FROM THE PUBLIC TELEVISION SERIES
HOSTED BY MARCEL DESAULNIERS AND CAROLYN O'NEIL
weber
Cascade
COMPLETE
M
PP
641.5973
C7713
Ma

CONTENTS

INTRODUCTION

For many, state fairs, large neighborhood and family picnics, and harvest celebrations conjure up images of the past that have faded away in an era of fast food and fast living. But look deeper and you will see they have not faded away but are still alive, just in the slightly different form of food festivals. In the last 20 years, culinary celebrations have sprouted up all over the country, drawing tens of thousands of people who come to spend a day tasting delicious foods, relaxing in the sun, having fun, and listening to music. Many of the organizers of festivals we visited were also surprised at the way their festivals have grown and how food—the centerpiece of the festival—continued to be the number one draw for the culinary curious who are eager to discover new tastes.

This cookbook contains recipes from 24 food festivals, described here, which we visited in the third season of the public television series, *Cook-Off America.* The food festivals presented a truly delightful mix, celebrating everything from eggplant and heirloom tomatoes to watermelon and coffee. This season we included visits to food celebrations that, while they didn't take place on American soil, represent important parts of our culinary melting pot. No matter where we went, from towns of 600 people to cities of millions, we found tremendous spirit and pride—and, of course, lots of great food.

Ghirardelli Chocolate Festival
San Francisco's Ghirardelli Square is the scene of a yearly extravaganza where thousands of people gather to celebrate what is probably the world's most beloved ingredient—chocolate. Dark, light, or white, it's found in everything from cakes, cookies, and pies to ice cream and candy. The San Francisco chocolate celebration offers up chocolate sculptures, chocolate eating contests, and the world's largest truffle.

Luling Watermelon Thump
Luling, a tiny town in Texas that looks like a movie set from an old-time western, is home to the famous Black Diamond watermelon. Every year, the town opens its door to thousands of visitors who spend the day munching on sweet, red, juicy watermelon or watching the watermelon eating contests and seed spitting contests.

Festival of Greece
If you can't go to Greece, the next best thing is a visit to one of the many Greek festivals held all over the United States, where you can spend the day listening to mesmerizing music and eating an unending offering of divine food befitting any Greek god. We found a terrific festival in the beautiful hills of Oakland, California, overlooking the San Francisco Bay area.

Aspen Food and Wine Classic
If your idols wear toques and white jackets and spend the majority of their time in the kitchen, the Aspen Food and Wine Classic is just where you want to be. It's a gathering of some of the top chefs in the country who present the latest trends in food and wine and take all participants one notch higher on the culinary ladder.

Kona Coffee Cultural Festival
The Kona region of Hawaii is considered by many to grow some of the best coffee beans in the world in its volcanic, mineral-rich soil. The locals' pride in their distinguished coffee shows through at the annual Kona Coffee Cultural Festival, which attracts coffee lovers from around the world.

Mendocino Crab and Wine Days
Starting in December, Mendocino Cape, which runs along the beautiful, picturesque northern coast of California, produces over ten million pounds of Dungeness crab yearly. The Mendocino Crab and Wine Days is a celebration held every January where visitors can enjoy both the crab and the area's renowned wines or go crab fishing.

Bite of Seattle
The Pacific Northwest has a profusion of wonderful local ingredients, from salmon and wild berries to mushrooms and crab. It also has an abundance of talented chefs whose creations can be sampled every July at Bite of Seattle. One of the largest food festivals in the U.S., it attracts millions of people from all over the country.

Jamaica Spice Festival
Jamaica's not just about lazy days on breezy beaches and evenings dancing to the hypnotic beat of local music—it's also about great food with exciting, bold, and spicy flavors. The yearly Jamaican Spice Festival is the place to go to try authentic Jamaican food and learn how to prepare it.

Bacardi Recipe Classic
Johnson and Wales University alumni submit their finest culinary creations for top prizes at the Bacardi Recipe Classic. The annual assembly of food service professionals is a sight to behold as they vie for the chance to display their craft using Bacardi rum products.

Riverside County Fair and National Datefest
Riverside County in the California desert valley holds a yearly celebration honoring one of the oldest and most venerable crops in the world—dates. Thousands of visitors converge upon this oasis of dates, tasting an abundant sampling of date foods and learning about this fascinating fruit of the date palm.

North Beach Festival
In the North Beach neighborhood of San Francisco (its "Little Italy"), the spirit of

Italian cuisine is felt in every restaurant, store, and sidewalk café. It's celebrated every June at the North Beach Festival, the oldest urban street fair in the country where visitors can roam the streets sampling the best of the Italian restaurants and markets.

Utica Old-Fashioned Ice Cream Festival

Summer kicks off with "a lick and a slurp" in dairy country, as the residents of Utica, Ohio, host a grand celebration in honor of America's most beloved treat. The annual Old-Fashioned Ice Cream Festival serves up plenty of fun with everything from water balloon tosses to ice cream eating contests.

U.S. Army Culinary Classic

When it comes to U.S. Army cooking, canned, tasteless food is a thing of the past. The military's efforts to give soldiers fresh, high-quality, nutritional meals are highlighted in an annual competition where army chefs battle one another to win culinary gold.

Singapore Food Festival

With an abundance of restaurants and array of cuisines, it is no wonder why "eating" is Singapore's national pastime. A stunning range of cuisine can be found throughout city streets including Chinese, Indian, and Malay. The nation boasts thousands of eateries that tantalize even the most discerning of palates.

Courtland Pear Fair

The Delta region of California near Sacramento is famous for its pears, which thrive on the area's cool breezes and rich soil. The 600 residents of Courtland, most of whom come from pear-farming families, open their doors every summer to anyone who would like to share their celebration of the first pear harvest by eating pear pie, pear fritters, and other pear foods.

Lambtown USA

The town of Dixon, California, is the center of historic community of lamb ranchers who take great pride in their profession. Their yearly celebration, called "Lambtown USA," is a weekend of festivities that includes lamb shearing contests, parades, displays of beautiful wools, and lots of mouthwatering lamb dishes.

Oktoberfest

Munich plays center stage to the largest—and one of the oldest—public festivals in the world. The Oktoberfest has been a lively tradition of merriment for over a century. Each year, more than six million visitors congregate in the heart of Bavaria to enjoy great music, superior beer, and enticing cuisine at this world-renowned celebration of immense proportions.

Isleton Crawdad Festival

Isleton, California, a small, quiet river town of just 850 people, swells to more than 200,000 during the annual Isleton Crawdad

Festival. Over three days, this ever-popular celebration cooks up more than 22,000 pounds of crawdads, the lesser-known cousin of lobster. Crawfish, crawdads, or mudbugs—by any name, these delicacies are heartily devoured.

Festival de la Familia

Latino cuisine offers a varied and eclectic mix of dishes from Mexico, Guatemala, El Salvador, and Puerto Rico—just to name a few—and they're all available for tasting under one roof at the Festival de la Familia in Sacramento, California. Besides culinary delights, there's dynamic music and dancing and authentic arts and crafts.

Great Southern Food Festival

Southern food has a long, rich heritage with imprints from the many different cultures of people who settled there and the bountiful ingredients found there. The cuisine is celebrated every year on the streets of Memphis, where visitors can eat a slice of the South, whether their passion is for fried chicken, grits, pecan pie, jambalaya, or fried green tomatoes.

Taste of Chicago

The Windy City celebrates a longtime tradition of culinary distinction with the legendary Taste of Chicago. More than three million visitors descend upon the city streets to sample a dazzling array of the best fare Chicago has to offer. From local specialties to ethnic cuisine, there is something for every taste bud.

Hayward Zucchini Festival

Hayward, California, a normally unnoticed sleepy suburban community outside San Francisco, comes alive every fall at their annual zucchini festival, which attracts tens of thousands of visitors who find zucchini in all sizes and shapes—from two inches to two feet long and weighing two ounces to two pounds. Booth after booth at the festival offers tastes of zucchini in a variety of forms: fried, steamed, baked, or blended.

Loomis Eggplant Festival

If you don't know whether eggplant is a vegetable or fruit or who brought the first plant to America, you haven't been to the Loomis Eggplant Festival in California where eggplants rule for the day. It's found in a wonderful sampling of dishes that visitors can try while enjoying a myriad of fun activities.

TomatoFest

What began in Carmel, California, as a small gathering for friends and family has blossomed into the annual TomatoFest, an extravagant display of the best heirloom tomatoes in the nation. Lucky attendees get to taste a staggering showcase of different varieties and taste favorite heirloom tomato recipes prepared by some of California's top chefs.

CHOCOLATE HEART OF DARKNESS CAKES

Ghirardelli Chocolate Festival

Our co-host of the series, Marcel Desaulniers, provided this recipe from one of his exquisite cookbooks, *Death By Chocolate Cakes* (William Morrow & Co., 2000). The molten centers make for an enthralling experience. They can be refrigerated up to 4 days and reheated one or two at a time for 30 to 40 seconds on the Defrost setting in a microwave oven.

Makes 12 cakes

Dark Chocolate Truffle Hearts

8 ounces semisweet baking chocolate, coarsely chopped
3/4 cup heavy cream

Chocolate Cocoa Cakes

5 ounces (10 tablespoons) unsalted butter, cut into 1-tablespoon pieces, plus 2 teaspoons melted
2/3 cup all-purpose flour
1/2 cup unsweetened cocoa powder
8 ounces semisweet baking chocolate, coarsely chopped
3 large eggs
2 large egg yolks
1/2 cup sugar
1 teaspoon pure vanilla extract

To make the Truffle Hearts: Place chopped semisweet chocolate in a small bowl. Heat heavy cream in a small saucepan over medium heat. Bring to a boil. Pour the boiling cream over the chopped chocolate. Set aside for 5 minutes and then stir with a whisk until smooth. Pour the mixture (called *ganache*) onto a nonstick baking sheet and use a rubber spatula to spread the ganache in a smooth, even layer to within 1 inch of the inside edges. Place the ganache in the freezer for 15 minutes, or in the refrigerator for 30 minutes, until very firm to the touch.

Line a 10- to 12-inch dinner plate with parchment paper or waxed paper. Remove the firm ganache from the freezer or refrigerator. Portion 12 heaping tablespoons (a bit more than 1 ounce each) of ganache onto the paper. Wearing disposable vinyl (or latex) gloves, individually roll each portion of the ganache in your palms in a circular motion, using just enough gentle pressure to form a smooth orb. Return each formed truffle to the paper-lined plate, and place in the freezer while preparing the cake batter.

To make the Chocolate Cocoa Cakes: Preheat the oven to 325 degrees F. Lightly coat the inside of each of 12 individual nonstick muffin cups (3 inches in diameter) with some of the 2 teaspoons melted butter. Set aside until needed.

In a sifter, combine the flour and cocoa powder. Sift onto a large piece of parchment paper or waxed paper, and set aside until needed.

Melt chopped semisweet chocolate and the remaining 5 ounces butter in the top half of a double boiler or in a microwave oven, and stir until smooth.

Place eggs, egg yolks, and sugar in the bowl of an electric stand mixer fitted with a paddle. Beat on medium-high speed for 2 minutes until the mixture is slightly frothy. Add the melted chocolate and butter and mix on low speed to combine, about 15 seconds. Continue on low while gradually adding the sifted dry ingredients. Once they are incorporated, stop the mixer and scrape down the sides of the bowl. Add the vanilla extract and mix on medium, about 15 seconds. Remove the bowl from the mixer and use a rubber spatula to mix the batter until thoroughly combined.

Portion 3 heaping tablespoons (about 2½ ounces each) of the cake batter into each muffin cup. On the center rack of the oven, bake cakes for 5 minutes. Remove the truffles from the freezer. Remove the muffin tin from the oven and quickly place a single frozen truffle in the center of each cake, pressing the truffle about halfway down into the batter. Return the muffin tin to the center rack of the oven and bake until a toothpick inserted into the cake (not the truffle) comes out clean, 17 to 18 minutes.

Remove the cakes from the oven and cool at room temperature for 20 minutes. To remove the cakes from the muffin cups, hold the top edge of the cake and give the cake a slight jiggle to loosen it from inside the cup. Then insert the pointed tip of a knife into an outside edge of the top of the cake and loosen it so you can gently pull the baked cake out of the cup. Serve immediately while still warm.

Cover the cooled cakes with plastic wrap for up to 24 hours at room temperature, or in the refrigerator for 3 to 4 days. Rewarm them in a microwave oven, 1 or 2 at a time, for 30 to 40 seconds on Defrost power.

SAN FRANCISCO
PREMIUM
QUALITY
GHIRARDELLI
FOUNDED 1852
Ghirardelli

SPRING WATERMELON SALAD WITH CITRUS VINAIGRETTE

Luling Watermelon Thump

This makes a wonderful summer salad that juxtaposes the crisp sweetness of watermelon with a salad that's dressed with Asian flavors. It goes especially well with grilled fish or chicken. Don't forget to toast the sesame seeds in either an oven or sauté pan; toasted sesame seeds add a great dimension of flavor to the salad.

Makes 6 servings

6 cups watercress (leaves and tops of stems)
4 cups cubed watermelon (about 1/2-inch cubes, seeds removed)
1/2 cup chopped green onion
1/2 cup fresh chervil leaves (optional)
1/4 cup coarsely chopped flat-leaf parsley
1/2 teaspoon sesame oil
3 tablespoons sesame seeds
1/3 cup Citrus Vinaigrette

Citrus Vinaigrette
1/2 cup olive oil
1/2 cup peanut oil
3 tablespoons minced shallot
2 tablespoons rice wine vinegar
2 tablespoons cider vinegar
1 tablespoon orange juice
1 tablespoon lemon juice
1 tablespoon lime juice
2 teaspoons coarse-grain Dijon mustard
1 teaspoon honey

Toss watercress, watermelon, green onion, chervil, and parsley in a large bowl; set aside. Heat sesame oil in a small skillet; add sesame seeds. Cook over low heat, stirring, until

sesame seeds just begin to darken. Remove from the heat and stir; toss with the watermelon mixture. Cover with plastic wrap and refrigerate until ready to serve.

Place all the vinaigrette ingredients in the container of an electric blender or food processor. Cover and pulse until smooth. Store in the refrigerator. (The vinaigrette may also be whisked by hand in a medium bowl.) This recipe makes $2\frac{1}{2}$ cups.

To serve, drizzle $\frac{1}{3}$ cup Citrus Vinaigrette over salad; toss to coat. Serve at once.

MAD'S SENSATIONAL WATERMELON SALMON SKEWERS

Luling Watermelon Thump

If you never tried grilling watermelon, it's a real treat—especially when it's paired with salmon that has soaked up the flavors of the delicious marinade found in this recipe. This is a unique creation by watermelon spokesman Jon Ashton (also known as the "Mad Chef").

Makes 8 servings

1 pound boneless, skinless salmon fillet, cut lengthwise into 1/2-inch-wide strips
6 cups diced watermelon
16 wooden skewers, soaked in water
1 (1-inch) piece fresh ginger, peeled and chopped
1/2 cup mirin (Japanese rice wine)
1/4 cup sake
1/4 cup light soy sauce
1/4 cup watermelon juice (seeds removed)
2 tablespoons rice vinegar
2 tablespoons sesame seeds
Salt and freshly ground black pepper

Thread the salmon and the watermelon cubes onto the soaked skewers. In a blender, combine the ginger, mirin, sake, soy sauce, watermelon juice, rice vinegar, and 1 tablespoon of the sesame seeds and blend this marinade until smooth. Marinate fish for 2 hours to 2 days in the refrigerator.

Preheat the grill to medium high. Season the skewers with salt and pepper. Grill the salmon skewers for about 3 to 4 minutes. Turn the skewers over and continue cooking for 4 to 5 minutes more. Remove the skewers from the grill and serve immediately.

WATERMELON SORBET

Luling Watermelon Thump

Watermelon lovers will appreciate this no-fat dessert with its fresh, cool flavors. For extra pizzazz, serve in a martini glass with a fresh sprig of mint. For more wonderful watermelon recipes, visit the National Watermelon Promotion Board website at www.watermelon.org.

Makes about 9 cups

1/2 medium watermelon, sliced lengthwise
1 (6-ounce) can frozen pink lemonade concentrate, thawed and undiluted
1 (15 1/4-ounce) can crushed pineapple, undrained
1/2 cup sugar
Fresh mint sprigs, for garnish

Scoop out the watermelon flesh and place it in a blender or food processor. Process until smooth. Pour the purée through a fine-mesh strainer into a bowl, discarding the pulp and seeds. Measure 8 cups of the strained juice and place it in a large bowl. Add the lemonade concentrate, pineapple, and sugar, stirring until the sugar dissolves.

Pour the watermelon mixture into a 9 by 13-inch pan. Cover and freeze until firm. Break the frozen mixture into chunks. Place half the mixture in a blender or food processor and process until smooth. Repeat with the remaining frozen mixture. Scoop out into dessert bowls, garnish with mint sprigs, and serve immediately.

PRASSOPITA (LEEK AND FETA CHEESE PIE)

Festival of Greece

Here's a classic Greek dish that combines the savory sweet flavor of sautéed leeks with the tangy fresh flavor of feta cheese. Don't feel guilty about using frozen phyllo dough—not even professional chefs attempt to make their own. Remember to keep the dough under a moist towel as you prepare the layers.

Makes 8 to 12 servings

$1\frac{1}{2}$ pounds leeks, thinly sliced
1 tablespoon olive oil
$1\frac{1}{2}$ teaspoons chopped fresh thyme
$\frac{1}{2}$ bunch flat-leaf parsley, chopped
$\frac{1}{4}$ cup chopped fresh dill
Salt and freshly ground black pepper
4 ounces feta cheese, crumbled
$\frac{1}{4}$ cup grated Parmesan cheese
2 large eggs, beaten
$\frac{1}{2}$ package phyllo dough
Melted butter, for brushing

Preheat oven to 350 degrees F. In a large skillet over medium-high heat, cook the leeks in the oil for 10 minutes. Add herbs, salt, and pepper. Mix the cheeses with the eggs. Add this mixture to the leeks and mix well. Pour into a pan lined with 8 or 9 sheets phyllo, then top with 8 or 9 more phyllo sheets, buttering each layer. Lightly score the top. Bake for 1 hour.

Remove the Prassopita from the oven and allow to cool for 5 minutes at room temperature. Use a serrated knife to cut it into 8 to 12 equal portions and serve.

SOUVLAKIA

Festival of Greece

This well-loved dish, found in nearly every Greek restaurant, contains all of the signature ingredients of Greek cooking: lemon, oregano, olive oil, and garlic.

Makes 4 servings

1 1/2 pounds boneless lamb or pork, cut into 1/2-inch cubes
1/4 cup red wine or lemon juice
3 tablespoons olive oil
1 tablespoon dried oregano
Pinch thyme
2 cloves garlic, minced
2 white onions, quartered
4 tomatoes, quartered
2 to 3 green bell peppers, seeded and cut into 1 1/2-inch squares
Salt and freshly ground black pepper

Combine meat, red wine, olive oil, oregano, thyme, and garlic; cover and refrigerate to marinate several hours or overnight. Reserve marinade. Slip meat onto skewers alternately with the vegetables. Season with salt and pepper. Broil in the oven or barbecue over slow-burning coals for 12 to 15 minutes, turning occasionally to prevent burning. Brush with marinade while cooking. Remove the skewers from the oven or grill and serve immediately.

DOLMATHES (STUFFED GRAPE LEAVES)

Festival of Greece

These are a very popular treat in Greece and not difficult to make at home. They are eaten with your fingers and make a wonderful appetizer.

Makes about 40 appetizers

30 to 60 grapevine leaves, fresh or canned
3 onions, chopped
1/4 cup oil
3 cups rice, rinsed
Juice of 2 lemons
Salt and freshly ground black pepper to taste
1/2 cup each chopped parsley, dill, and mint
4 cups water
2 tablespoons each pine nuts and raisins (optional)
Lemon wedges, for garnish

Scald fresh leaves by leaving them in hot or boiling water for a few minutes. Rinse and drain. Rinse canned leaves in cold water. In a large skillet over medium-high heat, sauté onions in 1 tablespoon oil until golden brown, about 10 to 12 minutes. Add washed rice, juice of 1 lemon, salt, pepper, parsley, dill, mint, and 1 cup water. Cover and simmer 10 minutes. Mix in pine nuts and raisins. Stuff 1 leaf at a time: Spread a grape leaf, dull side up, flat on a plate. Place 1 teaspoon or tablespoon (depending on the size of the leaf) of stuffing on the center of the leaf. Turn up stem end of leaf; then 1 at a time, fold over each side to enclose the stuffing completely. Starting at the stem end, roll grape leaf gently but firmly into a compact cylinder. Surfaces of the leaf will cling together. Place 2 or 3 coarse leaves on the bottom of a heavy saucepan. Arrange stuffed leaves side by side in layers. Add 3 cups water, the remaining 3 tablespoons oil, a little salt, and the juice of 1 lemon. Place a few more coarse leaves on top. Cover with a heavy plate to hold dolmathes in place. Cover pan and simmer 30 to 40 minutes, until all water is absorbed. Uncover and allow to cool. To serve, arrange stuffed grape leaves attractively on a platter or individual plates. Garnish with lemon wedges.

TOMATO TARTE TATIN

Aspen Food and Wine Classic

This recipe, which comes from New York City's star chef Daniel Boulud, has a layer each of sweet, caramelized onions, roasted tomatoes, and herbed goat cheese sandwiched between puff pastry. While there are several components, each one is easy to assemble and the final results are well worth the effort as an appetizer for a dinner party.

Makes 4 servings

Tomatoes
10 plum tomatoes, sliced crosswise 1/8 inch thick
2 tablespoons extra virgin olive oil
Salt and freshly ground black pepper to taste

Puff Pastry
1/2 pound puff pastry
1 egg, whisked with 1 teaspoon water

Caramelized Onions
1 tablespoon unsalted butter
4 cups peeled and thinly sliced onions
Salt and freshly ground black pepper

Herbed Goat Cheese
2 tablespoons goat cheese
1 teaspoon mascarpone cheese
1 teaspoon heavy cream
Extra virgin olive oil
1 tablespoon finely chopped shallot
1 tablespoon finely chopped chives
2 thyme sprigs, leaves only, finely chopped
1/2 teaspoon finely chopped garlic
Salt and freshly ground black pepper to taste

Pesto Sauce
2 bunches basil, leaves only, washed
1/2 clove garlic, peeled and germ removed
1 teaspoon pine nuts, very lightly toasted
1 teaspoon finely grated Parmesan cheese
3/4 cup extra virgin olive oil

Frisée Salad
1 cup frisée, white and yellow parts only, trimmed, washed, and dried
3 white mushrooms, thinly sliced
1 tablespoon chervil leaves
4 chive stems, cut into 1/4-inch pieces
2 tablespoons extra virgin olive oil, plus more for drizzling
3 teaspoons lemon juice
Cherry tomatoes, halved, for garnish (optional)

To make the tomatoes: Preheat the oven to 300 degrees F. In four 4-inch-round nonstick pans, arrange a pinwheel of tomato slices, overlapping them slightly. Make a second pinwheel of tomato slices in the center so that the bottom of the pan is completely covered. Sprinkle with the olive oil and season with salt and pepper.

Set the pans on a baking sheet and bake for 30 to 40 minutes. The tomatoes should be very soft. Using the back of a spoon, press down on the tomatoes until very flat.

To make the puff pastry: Increase the oven temperature to 375 degrees F. Roll out the puff pastry to about 1/8 inch thick and cut out 4 disks with a 4-inch-round cookie cutter. Place the disks on a baking pan lined with parchment paper. Refrigerate the disks for 15 minutes.

Brush the tops with the egg wash, and using the tines of a fork, prick the dough all over. Bake the disks for about 8 to 10 minutes, or until golden brown.

To make the onions: Melt the butter in a large pan over medium-low heat. Add the onions and season with salt and pepper. Cook until the onions begin to brown, about 10 to 15 minutes. Continue cooking until well browned, transfer to a plate, and set aside.

To make the goat cheese: In a small bowl, mix the goat and mascarpone cheeses, heavy cream, olive oil, shallots, chives, thyme, and garlic. Season with salt and pepper.

To make the pesto: Bring a pot of water to boil over high heat. Plunge the basil into the boiling water and blanch for 2 minutes. Drain the leaves and refresh under cold water. Let cool. Drain again, and squeeze the leaves free of excess moisture. Put all of the ingredients into a food processor and purée until smooth. Transfer to a bowl and cover, pressing a piece of plastic wrap against the surface. Set aside until needed.

To make the salad and assemble: In a medium bowl, toss the frisée with the mushrooms, chervil, chives, 2 tablespoons olive oil, and lemon juice. Place a layer of the soft herbed goat cheese over the tomatoes in their pans. Drizzle some of the pesto sauce over the goat cheese. Place a layer of the caramelized onions over the goat cheese and top with a puff pastry circle. Place the pans on a sheet pan and bake in the oven until the tarts are warm.

Flip each pan over onto the center of a plate. With a spoon, gently tap the bottom of the pans to release the tart. Remove the pans. Place a small mound of the frisée salad on top. Drizzle some olive oil and pesto around the plate. Garnish with cherry tomato halves, if desired.

BUTTERMILK-BACON SMASHED POTATOES

Aspen Food and Wine Classic

Manhattan-born chef Bobby Flay has perfected this spin on one of America's tried-and-true favorites. The extra step of roasting garlic lends a splendid flavor that is unbeatable.

Makes 4 servings

4 pounds Red Bliss potatoes, quartered
2 tablespoons salt plus extra to taste
1/2 cup (1 stick) unsalted butter, softened
1 1/2 cups buttermilk
4 cloves roasted garlic, peeled and mashed to a paste
8 slices cooked bacon, crumbled
Freshly ground black pepper to taste

Place the potatoes in a large saucepan, cover with cold water and add 2 tablespoons of salt. Bring to a boil and cook until tender. Drain well and place back in the pan over low heat.

Add the butter, buttermilk, and garlic and mash until smooth. Fold in the bacon, season with salt and pepper, and serve.

BLUE CORN–FRIED CHICKEN WITH ANCHO-HONEY SAUCE

Aspen Food and Wine Classic

Buttermilk has always been considered an excellent tenderizer for chicken and is often found in fried chicken recipes. This recipe from the renowned Southwestern chef Bobby Flay has a unique twist with its use of blue cornmeal.

Makes 4 servings

Ancho-Honey Sauce
1 cup honey
2 tablespoons ancho chile powder

Fried Chicken
1 whole chicken (3 to 4 pounds), cut into 8 pieces
3 cups buttermilk
Peanut oil, for frying
Salt and freshly ground black pepper
2 cups all-purpose flour, seasoned with salt and pepper
4 large eggs, lightly whisked
3 cups blue cornmeal, seasoned with salt and pepper

In a bowl, mix the honey with the chile powder until blended.

Place chicken in a large baking dish, add the buttermilk, turn to coat. Cover and place in the refrigerator for at least 4 hours.

Heat 1 inch of peanut oil in a cast-iron skillet until it registers 350 degrees F on a deep-frying thermometer. Remove the chicken from the buttermilk, pat dry, and season with salt and pepper. Dredge each piece of chicken in the flour, shake off any excess, then dip in the eggs, and then the cornmeal. Working in batches, slowly add the chicken pieces to the hot oil, skin side down. Cover the skillet and reduce the heat to medium-high; cook for 7 minutes. Remove the cover, turn the chicken over, and continue to cook for 6 to 7 minutes. Drain on paper towels and transfer to a platter. Drizzle with the Ancho-Honey Sauce and serve with Buttermilk-Bacon Smashed Potatoes (see opposite page).

KONA COFFEE KEBABS

Kona Coffee Cultural Festival

This recipe by Bill and Lianne Magness won third place at the Kona Coffee Cultural Festival held yearly in Hawaii. Kona coffee beans, grown in the rich volcanic soil of Hawaii where some of the best coffee beans in the world are produced, add a new dimension to this beef marinade.

Makes 4 servings

Marinade
2 cups 100% Kona coffee (strong brew)
1 cup firmly packed brown sugar
2 tablespoons honey mustard
2 tablespoons mustard
1 tablespoon Worcestershire sauce
1/2 cup lemon juice
1/4 teaspoon hot pepper sauce
2 teaspoons minced garlic
1 teaspoon cornstarch

2 pounds beef loin strips, cut into 1-inch cubes
2 red bell peppers, cut in 3/4- to 1-inch dice
1 red onion, cut in 3/4- to 1-inch dice
20 cherry tomatoes

In a medium saucepan over medium-high heat, bring the coffee, brown sugar, mustards, Worcestershire sauce, lemon juice, hot pepper sauce, and garlic to a boil. Pour out 1/4 cup of the coffee mixture into a small bowl or measuring cup and mix in the cornstarch. Return the cornstarch mixture to the pan, bring it back to a boil, and boil for 5 minutes. Let cool.

Thread the beef cubes onto skewers. Also, on separate skewers, thread the peppers, onion, and cherry tomatoes. Skewer each item separately as cooking times vary. Grill over low heat, turning and basting with the marinade for 20 to 30 minutes or until done.

KONA COFFEE–CRUSTED RACK OF LAMB WITH TRUFFLE TARO MASH, PINEAPPLE PEACH CHUTNEY, AND WILD BERRY COFFEE JUS

Kona Coffee Cultural Festival

Here's a recipe by Ke'o Velasquez that won first place in the Kona coffee recipe contest held every year in Hawaii. The coffee crust gives the lamb both a beautiful color and excellent flavor.

Makes 5 servings

Truffle Taro Mash

2 cups chopped Yukon Gold potatoes, boiled
2 cups cubed taro, steamed
1/4 cup (1/2 stick) butter (adjust to personal taste)
1/2 cup heavy whipping cream, heated
3 tablespoons truffle oil
Salt and freshly ground black pepper to taste

Kona Coffee Crust

1/2 cup Kona coffee grounds
1/4 cup minced thyme
1/4 cup minced rosemary
2 tablespoons minced parsley
1 tablespoon freshly ground black pepper
1 tablespoon kosher salt

1/4 cup vegetable oil
2 racks of lamb, about 2 pounds each, cleaned and fat removed
Pineapple Peach Chutney (see page 34)

Berry Jus
1/2 cup chopped carrots
1/2 cup chopped celery
1 cup chopped onions
2 tablespoons vegetable oil
3 cups red wine
5 cups lamb stock, cooked down to 1 1/2 cups (or to desired thickness)
1/2 cup brewed Kona coffee
4 bay leaves
1 tablespoon peppercorns
4 thyme sprigs
1/2 cup fresh raspberries (or any berry of your choice)
1/2 cup blackberry jam
Salt and freshly ground black pepper (optional)

To make the mash: Rice both potatoes and taro into separate bowls. Incorporate butter and cream into the potato mash; season with salt and pepper. Gently fold in the taro mash and truffle oil until just mixed. Adjust seasonings. Set aside.

To prepare the lamb: Preheat the grill to medium-high. Mix the Kona Coffee Crust ingredients together in a small bowl. Generously rub the lamb racks with 2 tablespoons of the oil. Use your hands to rub the coffee crust on the lamb until the meat is evenly coated (not all of the coffee crust will adhere).

Grill the lamb on both sides quickly to slightly char the outside. Transfer the lamb to the upper rack of the grill to cook, turning occasionally to prevent burning. Cook the lamb racks until they reach an internal temperature of 120 degrees F, about 20 minutes. (Cooking time will vary with individual grills.) Remove the lamb from the grill and allow to rest at room temperature while you make the jus.

To make the jus: Sauté vegetables in the oil until caramelized and golden brown. Pour in red wine and reduce until almost dry (no liquid). Pour in lamb stock and coffee. Add the bay leaf, peppercorns, and thyme sprigs. Simmer for 2 minutes. Add raspberries and blackberry jam. Reduce liquid to 1 cup. Strain the liquid through a fine-mesh strainer and add salt and pepper if desired.

To arrange: Place half of the Truffle Taro Mash in a piping bag and pipe onto individual plates in a round flower shape. Use a sharp knife to cut the racks into chops each with a bone. Serve 3 lamb chops next to the mash and add a vegetable of your choice. Drizzle 2 tablespoons or more of the chutney on top of the vegetables. Drizzle 2 tablespoons of the jus over and in front of the lamb.

GRAND
MARSHALL
BREAKFAST
LUNCH
KONA LE'A PLANTATION
HOLUALOA · HAWAII
HOLUALOA Coffee
Pure Kona
Hand Picked
FANCY

PINEAPPLE PEACH CHUTNEY

Kona Coffee Cultural Festival

This chutney makes a wonderful accompaniment to the Kona Coffee–Crusted Rack of Lamb or just about any grilled meat.

Makes about 3 1/2 cups

1/4 cup raisins
1/4 cup diced dried peaches
1/2 cup warm water
1 1/2 cups fresh pineapple cut into 1/4-inch cubes
1 cup fresh peaches cut into 1/4-inch cubes
1 cup diced Maui onions
2 cinnamon sticks
4 whole cloves
3 whole star anise
1/2 cup firmly packed brown sugar
1/2 cup cider vinegar
1 teaspoon sambal (Asian fresh ground chili paste)
1/4 cup minced fresh ginger
2 tablespoons minced garlic

Soak dried raisins and peaches in the warm water to soften. Mix remaining ingredients in a bowl. Place all ingredients in a medium sauté pan over medium heat and cook until the fruit is tender and the sugar begins to caramelize into a golden brown. Remove from the heat. Remove cinnamon sticks, cloves, and star anise. Set aside until ready to use. Store the chutney in a tightly sealed plastic container in your refrigerator.

KONA COFFEE LAND DREAM CREAM

Kona Coffee Cultural Festival

This delicious drink recipe by Beverly Behasa won first prize at the Kona Coffee Cultural Festival in the beverage category. It can be used to sweeten and cream hot coffee.

Makes 7 cups

2/3 cup firmly packed brown sugar
3/4 teaspoon cinnamon
2 teaspoons instant Kona coffee blend, freeze-dried
2 cups freshly brewed 100% Kona coffee
4 cups milk
1 tablespoon vanilla extract
1/2 pint whipping cream

Combine all ingredients. Chill well and serve. Try it over ice cream or as an addition to your hot coffee as a sweetener and creamer.

CRUMBLY PEANUT BUTTER KONA COFFEE COOKIES

Kona Coffee Cultural Festival

Here's a delightful cookie that joins the flavors of peanut butter and coffee. For a softer cookie, remove the cookies from the baking sheet soon after they come out of the oven. For a crisper cookie, allow them to sit on the baking sheet for a while.

Makes 2 dozen cookies

1/2 cup (1 stick) butter
1/2 cup firmly packed brown sugar
1/2 cup granulated sugar
1 egg
1/2 teaspoon salt
1/2 teaspoon baking soda
1 1/2 cups peanut butter, chunky or creamy
3 tablespoons instant Kona coffee granules
1 1/2 cups flour

Preheat the oven to 375 degrees F.

In a large bowl, cream the butter. Combine the sugars and mix gradually into the butter. Add the egg, salt, baking soda, peanut butter, and coffee granules. Blend until creamy. Sift and add the flour to the batter.

Roll the dough into balls or drop from a spoon onto an ungreased cookie sheet. Press each flat with a fork, making a criss-cross design. Bake for 15 minutes or until brown.

Velvet

CHOCOLATE COFFEE ICE CREAM PIE

Kona Coffee Cultural Festival

Here's a dream dessert: a chocolate crumb crust is first topped with mocha ice cream and then with a layer of ganache and crowned with chocolate covered coffee beans. The chocolate crumb crust can be made with store-bought chocolate wafers or make your own cookies from scratch.

Chocolate Cookie Crumble Crust

3 ounces semisweet baking chocolate, coarsely chopped
2 ounces unsweetened baking chocolate, coarsely chopped
3/4 cup all-purpose flour
1/2 teaspoon baking soda
1/4 teaspoon salt
1/2 cup (1 stick) unsalted butter, cut into 1/2-ounce pieces, plus 3 tablespoons (melted)
1/2 cup granulated sugar
1/2 cup (4 ounces) tightly packed light brown sugar
2 large eggs
1 1/2 teaspoons pure vanilla extract

Ice Cream Center

3/4 gallon coffee ice cream (your favorite)

Coffee Ganache

4 ounces semisweet baking chocolate, coarsely chopped
1/2 cup heavy whipping cream
2 tablespoons coffee liqueur

To make the crust: Preheat the oven to 325 degrees F. Melt the chopped semisweet chocolate and chopped unsweetened chocolate in the top half of a double boiler or in a small glass bowl in the microwave oven, and stir until smooth. Set aside until needed.

In a sifter combine the flour, baking soda, and salt. Sift onto a large piece of parchment paper (or waxed paper) and set aside until needed.

Place 1/2 cup butter, granulated sugar, and the light brown sugar in the bowl of an electric stand mixer fitted with a paddle. Mix on low speed for 1 minute, then beat on medium for 3 minutes until soft and thoroughly combined. Use a rubber spatula to scrape down the sides of the bowl. Add the eggs, one at a time, beating on medium for 30 seconds after each addition, and scraping down the sides of the bowl once both eggs have been incorporated. Beat on medium speed until very soft, about 2 minutes. Add the melted chocolate and mix on medium for 15 seconds; then scrape down the sides of the bowl. Lower the speed to low, and while gradually adding the sifted dry ingredients, mix until incorporated, about 30 seconds. Add the vanilla extract and mix on medium to combine, about 10 seconds. Remove the bowl from the mixer and use a rubber spatula to finish mixing the ingredients until thoroughly combined.

Using 3 slightly heaping tablespoons (approximately 2 ounces) or 1 heaping #20 ice cream scoop, portion the batter into 6 cookies, evenly spaced on 2 nonstick baking sheets. Place the baking sheets on the top and center racks of the preheated oven and bake for 35 minutes, rotating the sheets from top to center halfway through the baking time (at that time also turn each sheet 180 degrees). Remove the cookies from the oven and cool to room temperature on the baking sheets, about 10 minutes. Leave the oven on. Don't be dismayed by the baked appearance of the cookies—collapsed and wrinkled. Despite their looks, they are perfect for the cookie crust, crisp on the outside and moist in the center. Refrigerate the cookies for 15 minutes.

Break the chilled cookies into quarters, then place the quarters in a food processor fitted with a metal blade (depending on the size of your food processor, you may have to do this in two batches). Pulse the cookies until very fine, about 45 seconds. Add the 3 tablespoons of melted butter and pulse for 15 seconds. Transfer half the amount (2 1/4 cups) of crumbs to the inside bottom of a 1 3/4 by 9-inch springform pan. Spread the crumbs evenly over the bottom of the pan, then press firmly until smooth and even (wearing a pair of disposable vinyl or latex gloves makes this a much less messy job). Firmly press the remaining crumbs into the sides of the pan as evenly and uniformly as possible. Place on a baking sheet (this makes removing the pan from the oven easier) on the center rack of the preheated 325 degree F oven and bake for 12 minutes. Remove from the oven and cool at room temperature until needed.

To make the cake center: Place the ice cream in the bowl of an electric stand mixer fitted with a paddle. Mix on low speed for 30 seconds. Then increase the speed of the mixer to medium and mix until the ice cream appears to be the same texture as soft serve. Transfer the ice cream to the prepared cookie crust and smooth the top flat with a rubber spatula. Cover the top with plastic wrap and freeze until the ice cream is very hard, about 12 hours.

To prepare the ganache: After the ice cream cake has frozen for 12 hours, place the chopped semisweet chocolate in a medium bowl.

Heat the cream and coffee liqueur in a medium saucepan over medium-high heat. Bring to a boil. Pour the boiling cream over the chopped chocolate. Stir with a whisk until smooth. Then place the bowl in the refrigerator for 5 minutes to cool the ganache so that it will not melt the ice cream in the next step.

Remove the ice cream cake from the freezer and carefully remove and discard the plastic wrap. Pour the ganache (as long as you did not refrigerate for more than 5 minutes, the ganache should be pourable) onto the top of the frozen ice cream layer. Use a small offset or rubber spatula to spread the ganache evenly over the surface of the ice cream. Place the cake in the freezer for at least 1 hour before serving.

To serve, remove the cake from the freezer. Heat the blade of a serrated slicer under hot running water and wipe the blade dry before making each slice. Serve immediately and prepare yourself for the kudos, because this may be the most amazing ice cream cake your guests have ever enjoyed.

HOLUALOA MUD SLIDE KONA COFFEE CHOCOLATE CAKE

Kona Coffee Cultural Festival

Here's a rich, moist cake infused with coffee flavor and easy to prepare. Use good chocolate—nothing will happen in the oven to improve a bad-tasting chocolate.

Makes 10 to 12 servings

2 cups unbleached flour
1 teaspoon baking soda
¼ teaspoon salt
1¾ cup strongly brewed Kona coffee
¼ cups Kahlua or brandy
5 ounces unsweetened chocolate
1 cup (2 sticks) butter
2 cups sugar
2 eggs
1 teaspoon vanilla extract

Glaze (optional)
3 ounces semisweet chocolate
2 tablespoons brewed Kona coffee

Preheat oven to 275 degrees F. Butter a 10-inch Bundt pan and dust with cocoa. Sift together flour, baking soda, and salt. In a saucepan, heat coffee and liqueur on low for 5 minutes. Add chocolate and butter and stir until melted. When smooth, add sugar and stir until dissolved. Let the mixture cool several minutes. Transfer to a large bowl. Add flour mixture about half at a time, beating after each addition until smooth. Add eggs and vanilla. Beat for 1 minute. Pour batter into Bundt pan and bake for about 1½ hours, until cake pulls away from the sides of the pan and springs back when touched in the middle. Allow to cool in the pan for 10 minutes. Invert cake onto a plate. Remove pan when cake is completely cooled.

If desired, prepare glaze: In a small saucepan over low heat, melt the chocolate and coffee. Brush on the surface of the cooled cake.

OUR AWARD-WINNING CRAB CAKES AND CABBAGE SALAD

Mendocino Crab and Wine Days

This award-winning crab cake recipe leaves nothing to chance. Its creator, Nicholas Petti, uses his own homemade mayonnaise—a tarragon aioli—as a binder and the Japanese-style panko bread crumbs for a coating. The crunchy texture of these special bread crumbs, found in the Asian section of supermarkets, is excellent for seafood. Of course, if you're in a hurry, the crab cakes are still delicious with store-bought mayonnaise and regular bread crumbs.

Makes 4 servings

Tarragon Aioli

2 egg yolks
3 cloves garlic
Juice of 1 lemon
1/2 teaspoon salt
1 dash Tabasco sauce
1/4 cup very hot water
2 cups olive oil
1/2 bunch tarragon, finely chopped

Cabbage Salad

1 head green cabbage
Sea salt
1 bunch chives, finely chopped
1/3 cup champagne vinegar

Crab Cakes

1 1/2 pounds Dungeness crabmeat
3/4 cup panko bread crumbs plus extra for the outer coating
2 green onions, finely chopped
Oil for sautéing

To make the aioli: In food processor or blender, place the egg yolks, garlic, lemon juice, salt, and Tabasco sauce and blend. Pour in the hot water and process for 15 seconds. With machine running, slowly drizzle in oil until a mayonnaise consistency is reached. Stir in chopped tarragon.

To make the salad: Remove outer leaves and core from cabbage and slice thinly. Toss with a liberal amount of salt and let sit for 30 minutes. Drain off liquid from cabbage and add chives and vinegar. Refrigerate until needed.

To make the crab cakes: Combine crab, bread crumbs, and green onions. Add $^1/_2$ cup aioli and test mixture to see how well it holds together. If needed, add more aioli. Do not overwork ingredients. Cakes should be loose and just barely hold together. Form into cakes about 3 inches in diameter, and place one side in bread crumbs. Heat oil in medium sauté pan over medium-high heat until just smoking and place cakes, bread crumb side down, in pan. Sauté until golden and carefully turn over. Lower heat to medium and sauté until heated through. Serve on Cabbage Salad and top with additional aioli.

CRAB • SHRIMP
COCKTAILS
OYSTERS
CLAM CHOWDER
Best Crab & Wine Days
Crabcake
BISTRO

CRAB RICE PAPER ROLLS

Mendocino Crab and Wine Days

This recipe from California's well-known chef John Ash is a variation on the "California roll," which has become so popular in sushi restaurants. Instead of rice and nori, it uses cellophane noodles and edible rice paper; if you can't find these ingredients, you can substitute Boston lettuce leaves.

Makes 6 to 8 appetizer servings

2 ounces thin rice sticks or vermicelli
1 cucumber
2 firm ripe avocados
24 small rice paper rounds or quarter rounds, softened (see method following recipe)
1 pound cooked crabmeat
3 to 4 tablespoons drained sweet pickled ginger
1/2 cup finely sliced green onion or garlic chives
1/3 cup loosely packed mint or cilantro leaves
2 tablespoons lightly toasted sesame seeds

Dipping Sauce
1/4 cup fish sauce (nam pla)
5 tablespoons sugar
1/2 cup fresh lime juice
2 teaspoons finely minced garlic
2 teaspoons finely minced serrano or bird chiles (or to taste)

Soften the rice sticks in hot water for 10 minutes, then cook until tender in boiling water for a minute or so. Drain and rinse in cold water to stop cooking. Set aside, covered loosely in plastic wrap.

Peel and seed the cucumber and cut into 4-inch-long strips. Peel the avocado, discard pit, and cut into long slices.

For each roll, lay out a softened rice paper on a tea towel and place a tablespoon or so of the cooked rice stick across the center. Add a piece of cucumber, some of the crab, pickled ginger, green onion, avocado, and a mint leaf or two. Sprinkle with sesame seeds, fold the sides in, and then roll into a tight bundle.

To make the sauce: Heat the fish sauce and sugar in a small saucepan over low heat and stir till sugar is dissolved. Remove the pan from the heat and cool to room temperature. Stir in lime juice, garlic, and chiles and allow to sit for at least 1 hour before using. Can be made up to 2 days ahead and stored refrigerated. (Makes 1 cup.)

To serve: Place the crab rolls on a dish with the seam side down. Serve with dipping sauce. This is definitely a treat to eat with your fingers!

Softening Rice Papers

Traditionally the dry rice papers are dipped into a bowl of lukewarm water for 20 to 30 seconds or until they just begin to soften. Lay them out on a dry tea towel and let them sit for another minute or so until they are completely softened. You can usually do 4 to 6 at a time. An alternate method is to lay the rice papers between layers of damp towel, where they will soften in 5 to 8 minutes.

WASHINGTON'S OWN APPLE DUMPLINGS WITH APPLE CIDER SAUCE

Bite of Seattle

Here's a show-stopping fruit dessert, from Washington's Own Apple Dumpling Gang, which we found at Bite of Seattle festival. An apple baked with raisins and nuts is covered with a pastry topping that you can make from scratch or purchase premade. It's served with a warm Apple Cider Sauce and vanilla ice cream.

Makes 4 servings

Pastry Dough

1/4 cup high-gluten flour
1/2 teaspoon salt
1/8 teaspoon turmeric
1/4 cup vegetable shortening
1/2 cup (1 stick) unsalted butter
4 to 6 tablespoons ice water

Apple Filling

4 Washington Granny Smith apples
1 teaspoon cinnamon or to taste
1 teaspoon nutmeg or to taste
1 teaspoon sugar or to taste
1 teaspoon raisins (optional)
1 tablespoon brandy, apple jack, or rum (optional)
1 tablespoon pecans (optional)
1 large egg
1 tablespoon whole milk

Apple Cider Sauce

1 to 2 cups fresh apple cider
1 tablespoon cornstarch dissolved in 1 1/2 tablespoons warm water
1 tablespoon butter
Cinnamon and nutmeg to taste
Sugar to taste
1/4 cup raisins or to taste

To make the pastry: Combine flour, salt, turmeric, and shortening in the bowl of a food processor. Cut butter in 1/4-inch cubes into the bowl. Pulse until the dough resembles coarse meal. Transfer mixture to a mixing bowl and add ice water; work with a fork until it begins to pull away from the sides and form a ball. Add more water if necessary. Divide ball into 4 equal balls, wrap in plastic wrap, and refrigerate for 30 minutes.

Remove the dough balls from the refrigerator and allow them to come to room temperature. Roll out the dough balls on a floured surface and cut each into a 6- to 7-inch square (depending on size of apples).

To make the filling: Peel and core the apples. It's best to leave them whole and use a coring and peeling machine. (If you would like to prepare apples first, have a little fresh lemon available to squeeze over apples.) Place each apple in the center of a pastry square and sprinkle with the cinnamon, nutmeg, and sugar. You can fill the center with raisins, brandy, and pecans, if you so desire. Combine the egg and milk in a small bowl. Vigorously whisk this mixture with a fork until well combined. Fold 2 edges of the pastry square up over the top of the apple and press together using the egg wash. Bring up the other 2 edges in the same way. Brush entire top of dumpling with the egg wash. Place on parchment-lined baking sheet and bake at 350 degrees F for 30 to 35 minutes (convection oven). Bake until golden brown.

To make the sauce: Pour apple cider in a medium saucepan. Gently warm on very low heat. Add dissolved cornstarch. (Add more cornstarch if you like your sauce thicker.) Add butter, stirring constantly to allow butter to melt completely. Add cinnamon, nutmeg, sugar, and raisins. Allow sauce enough time to thicken and warm properly. Keep on low simmer until dumplings are ready to serve.

Remove dumplings from oven and allow to cool for about 5 minutes; place on dessert dishes and scoop old-fashioned vanilla ice cream on the side. Ladle a generous amount of Apple Cider Sauce over the apple and garnish with a sprinkle of nutmeg. Yum!

Note: The Dumpling Gang has used frozen puff pastry dough in the past. They turn out all right but the crust doesn't get as "crunchy" as it would with this dough. Also, the frozen puff pastry dough doesn't seem to hold up to the apples juices as well, and instead becomes wetter and absorbs more of the juice.

GRANNY SMITH–CRUSTED SALMON FILLET

Bite of Seattle

This simple, but creative and delicious recipe comes from Seattle chef Jay Sardeson. Granny Smiths are a preferred apple for cooking since they hold up well and don't turn mushy.

Makes 4 servings

1 tablespoon olive oil
4 (6-ounce) skinless salmon fillets
Salt and freshly ground black pepper
2 Granny Smith apples
1/4 cup mayonnaise
1/8 cup Dijon mustard
2 tablespoons Old Bay Seasoning
1 teaspoon freshly squeezed lemon juice
2 ounces blue cheese
1 teaspoon minced fresh ginger

Preheat the oven to 350 degrees F.

Brush a baking pan with olive oil and place salmon fillets in the pan. Season with salt and pepper. Peel, core, and shred the apples into a large bowl. Mix in mayonnaise, mustard, Old Bay Seasoning, lemon juice, blue cheese, and ginger. Top salmon fillet with apple mixture and bake for about 20 minutes, until the crust begins to brown around the edges and the salmon is slightly firm to the touch. Serve immediately.

CURRIED MUSSELS WITH SHIITAKE AND OYSTER MUSHROOMS

Bite of Seattle

Chefs Nan Wilkinson and Lil Miller of Pavé Bakery served this recipe at Bite of Seattle, a food festival held every year in July. The mussels are poached in a wine-water mixture and served with a highly flavored, creamy broth.

Makes 4 servings

32 mussels
2 cups plus 2 tablespoons water
2 cups wine
1 tablespoon olive oil
1 teaspoon chopped fresh Thai chiles
1 1/2 tablespoons grated fresh ginger
1 1/2 tablespoons chopped fresh garlic
1 1/2 tablespoons chopped fresh lemongrass
2 cups canned coconut milk
1 1/2 tablespoons fish sauce
2 tablespoons brown sugar
1/2 pound oyster mushrooms, sliced
1/2 pound shiitake mushrooms, sliced
6 green onions, chopped
4 teaspoons flour
2 tablespoons water
2 tablespoons chopped fresh basil

Poach mussels in 2 cups of the water and the wine; drain.

In a large saucepan over medium-high heat, heat the oil and sauté chiles, ginger, garlic, and lemongrass until tender, about 2 minutes. Stir in coconut milk, fish sauce, and brown sugar. Bring to a boil, then lower the heat and simmer, uncovered, about 2 to 3 minutes. Add mushrooms and cook 2 to 3 minutes until tender. Add green onions. Mix

the 2 tablespoons water and flour together, then slowly add this mixture to the sauce and simmer until thickened. Add mussels and warm them, but don't overcook! Add basil and serve immediately.

JAMAICA
KORG

PEPPERPOT SOUP

Jamaica Spice Festival

A big thank-you to the Walkerswood Company, which imports a wide range of Jamaican food products, for giving us this delicious, authentic soup recipe brimming with the flavors of Jamaican cuisine such as yam, cloves, and coconut milk. If you can't find Callaloo, substitute any cooking green such as spinach or collards.

Makes 4 to 6 servings

1/2 pound salted beef, cubed
1/2 pound braising beef, cubed
6 1/4 cups water
Salt
1 teaspoon whole cloves
1 fresh thyme sprig
2 (535g) cans Walkerswood Callaloo, drained
1/2 pound okra, cut into 3-inch pieces
1 (400ml) can Walkerswood Coconut Milk
1 large onion, thinly sliced
Freshly ground black pepper
1 whole Scotch bonnet pepper or a dash of Walkerswood Scotch Bonnet Pepper Sauce or Jonkanoo Pepper Sauce
3/4 pound yellow yams, peeled and cubed
2 cooked shell-on shrimp (prawns) for each bowl, for garnish (optional)

Place the salted beef and braising beef in a large saucepan with the water and some salt. Bring to the boil over high heat. Skim off fat that rises to the surface as necessary. Lower the heat and cook for 1 hour.

Add the remaining ingredients and bring back to a boil. Simmer for about 30 minutes, until the yam is soft. Adjust the seasoning. Garnish with the cooked shrimp and serve hot.

JAMAICAN JERK CHICKEN

Jamaica Spice Festival

This authentic jerk recipe comes right from Jamaica. The original Indian inhabitants of the Caribbean used to poke or "jerk" their meat before grilling to create holes to stuff with spices. The results create a wonderfully spiced, moist, and tender meat.

Makes 4 servings

1 Scotch bonnet or habanero pepper
1 medium chicken, about 3 1/2 pounds, quartered
1 tablespoon ground allspice
1 tablespoon dried thyme
1 1/2 teaspoons cayenne pepper
1 1/2 teaspoons freshly ground black pepper
1 1/2 teaspoons ground sage
3/4 teaspoon ground nutmeg
3/4 teaspoon ground cinnamon
2 tablespoons garlic powder or minced fresh garlic
1 tablespoon sugar
1/4 cup olive oil
1/4 cup soy sauce
3/4 cup white vinegar
1/2 cup orange juice
Juice of 1 lime
3 green onions, finely chopped
1 cup finely chopped onion

Seed and finely chop the Scotch bonnet pepper. Trim chicken of fat.

In a large bowl, combine the allspice, thyme, cayenne pepper, black pepper, sage, nutmeg, cinnamon, garlic powder, and sugar. With a wire whisk, slowly add the olive oil, soy sauce, vinegar, orange juice, and lime juice. Add the Scotch bonnet pepper, green onion, and onion, and mix well. Add the chicken breasts, cover, and marinate for at least 1 hour, longer if possible.

Preheat a grill to medium-high.

Remove the breasts from the marinade and grill for 6 minutes on each side or until cooked. While grilling, baste with the marinade. Heat the leftover marinade to a boil and set on the side for dipping.

Note: Scotch bonnet and habanero peppers are the hottest of the capsicum peppers—they're truly incendiary. Substitute serranos or Thai bird chiles if you can't find them.

SWEET POTATO PUDDING

Jamaica Spice Festival

Eva Henry-Hall won the Jamaican competition called "My Granny's Sweet Potato Pudding Contest" and was kind enough to share the recipe with us. Remember that yams and sweet potatoes are often confused and called different things in different regions. Yams have orange flesh and sweet potatoes have a white flesh. This is eaten as a dessert—not a side dish—in Jamaica.

Makes 8 to 12 servings

2 pounds sweet potatoes, washed, peeled, and boiled until fork-tender
3/4 pound yellow yams, washed, peeled, and boiled until fork-tender
1 quart coconut milk
3/4 cup cornmeal
1 1/2 cups flour
1 1/2 tablespoons butter
1 1/2 cups sugar
1/4 pound miscellaneous fruit (currants and raisins)
1 1/2 tablespoons vanilla extract
1 teaspoon nutmeg
2 teaspoons allspice
Pinch of salt
1 teaspoon cinnamon
1 1/2 teaspoons water

Preheat the oven to 350 degrees F. Purée sweet potatoes and yams in a blender or food processor. Remove to a bowl and stir in coconut milk, cornmeal, and flour. Add butter a little at a time, and then add sugar. Stir until the sugar is dissolved. Stir in currants, raisins, vanilla, nutmeg, allspice, and salt. If the pudding is too stiff, add coconut milk.

Butter a large casserole dish and dust with flour. Pour in sweet potato mixture. Cover with aluminum foil and bake for 1 1/2 hours. Combine the cinnamon and water in a small bowl. Remove the pudding from the oven, and with a pastry brush, brush the top of the pudding with the cinnamon water. Allow the pudding to set at room temperature and serve.

CARIBBEAN CALYPSO GRILLE

Bacardi Recipe Classic

This recipe with its fresh Caribbean flavors was one of the top prizewinners submitted by chef Stephen Pribish for the Bacardi Recipe Classic Contest, a competition for professional chefs at Johnson & Wales University.

Makes 4 to 6 servings

Fresh Caribbean-Rum Salsa

2 fresh pineapples, cored and finely diced
2 fresh mangoes, peeled and finely diced
2 red onions, finely diced
2 red bell peppers, finely diced
1 tablespoon freshly grated ginger
2 jalapeños, seeded and minced
1 tablespoon freshly chopped cilantro plus a few sprigs for garnish
4 ounces Bacardi Limon rum
Juice of 1 lime
Salt to taste

Beach Bum Rum Sauce

1 1/2 cups heavy cream
1 cup coconut milk
1 tablespoon granulated sugar
Kosher salt to taste
1 tablespoon cornstarch
1 cup Bacardi Tropico liqueur

Grille

10 to 12 U-15 (very large) shrimp
2 (1½-pound) pork tenderloin fillets
1 tablespoon paprika
½ teaspoon cayenne pepper
1 tablespoon garlic powder
2 teaspoons salt
1 tablespoon granulated sugar
1 teaspoon dried thyme

To make the salsa: Combine all ingredients in a large bowl. Cover and chill well.

To make the rum sauce: Put all ingredients except the rum into a small saucepan and bring to a simmer over medium heat. When the sauce begins to thicken enough to cling to the back of a spoon, take it off the heat and add the rum. Set aside.

To make the grilled meats: Peel, butterfly, and devein the shrimp, leaving the tails on. Clean the pork tenderloin of any excess fat or tough fibers. Mix all the dry ingredients together and sprinkle over the shrimp and pork.

Clean the grill grate and wipe it with a lightly oiled towel to keep the food from sticking.

Grill the pork over medium heat until it comes to an internal temperature of 150 degrees F, about 25 minutes. Remove the pork from the grill and allow it to rest.

Brush off the grill and add the shrimp. When the shrimp become bright orange-red and the flesh turns opaque white, about 1½ to 2 minutes on each side, remove them from the grill.

To serve: Spoon 2 tablespoons rum sauce in the middle of individual plates. Add ¼ cup salsa to the middle of the plate. Slice the grilled pork into 2-ounce medallions and place them on the plate. Place the shrimp on the pork and serve.

BACA
SUPER
TROPICO

TROPICO SUMMER FRUIT ROLLS

Bacardi Recipe Classic

This is a stunning dessert with a delicious pastry cream, fruit cooked in rum, and a raspberry sauce all served in a pastry shell—another award-winning recipe submitted by Michelle Tucker. Don't be afraid to use the frozen pastry shells found in supermarkets—many of them are very high quality.

Makes 10 servings

10 frozen puff pastry shells
2 cups whole milk
1½ cups cream of coconut
½ cup plus 3 tablespoons sugar
1 large egg
1 egg yolk
2 tablespoons all-purpose flour
1 tablespoon butter
½ cup shredded coconut, for garnish
1 large mango
2 large ripe peaches
¾ cup plus 6 tablespoons Bacardi Tropico or your favorite rum
1 cup fresh blueberries
1½ to 2 pints fresh raspberries
Confectioner's sugar for dusting

Preheat oven to 400 degrees F.

Arrange the puff pastry discs on an ungreased cookie sheet and allow to thaw slightly while preparing the custard.

In a 2-quart saucepan, combine the milk, ½ cup cream of coconut, and ½ cup granulated sugar. Set over medium heat. Place the egg and egg yolk in a separate bowl, sift the flour over the eggs, and then whisk until smooth (there should be no lumps of the flour in the eggs when finished).

Bake the puff pastry shells for 30 minutes. (If your oven takes longer to preheat, do this after the custard is finished.)

When the milk mixture is just beginning to boil, slowly ladle some of the hot liquid into the eggs and flour, whisking constantly. Add a total of about half the milk to the eggs. Lower the heat on the milk to medium-low and return the egg mixture to the pot, still whisking. Cook the custard until very thick and creamy, about 5 minutes. Remove from heat and mix in butter. Strain the custard through a mesh colander or other wide, stable strainer into a glass pie plate. Cover with plastic wrap, making sure the plastic touches the entire surface of the custard. Place the pie plate on the lowest shelf in your refrigerator and let cool.

In a saucepan, toast the 1/2 cup coconut until golden brown. Set aside and allow to cool.

Peel and slice the mango lengthwise into 1/4-inch-thick strips, then cut the strips in half lengthwise.

Peel and slice the peaches into sections (8 per peach), then cut the sections in quarters. If the peaches are a bit firm, cook them in a large saucepan with the 3/4 cup Tropico and 3 tablespoons sugar for a few minutes until softened slightly, then add the mango. If not, then cook them with the mango slices, 3 tablespoons sugar, and liqueur until heated through. Add blueberries and cook until all of the fruit is softened, but the blueberries are not "broken." Place in a bowl and set in the freezer, stirring occasionally to cool.

Mix together the remaining 1 cup cream of coconut and 6 tablespoons Tropico. Set aside.

In a small bowl, crush 1/2 cup raspberries with 2 to 3 tablespoons of the coconut and Tropico sauce. Set aside.

To assemble: With a knife or fork, remove the "tops" of the puff pastry discs and scoop out the flaky pastry in the center. Fill with the pastry cream.

Spoon about 2 tablespoons of the Tropico sauce on each plate and swirl to cover the base of the plate. Place the pastry discs in the center of each plate. Drop 3 to 4 very small spoonfuls of the raspberry sauce on each plate. Top the custard with the cooked fruit. Garnish the top with fresh raspberries, dust with confectioner's sugar, and serve.

SPICED CHICKEN AND DATE DELIGHT

Riverside County Fair and National Datefest

It's only natural to pair dates, an ancient fruit with roots in the Middle East, with the pungent and sweet flavors of Mediterranean cooking, which you find in this recipe.

Makes 2 servings

1/4 teaspoon ground cumin
1/4 teaspoon ground cinnamon
1/4 teaspoon ground coriander
1/4 teaspoon ground turmeric
1/4 teaspoon cayenne
2 (8-ounce) skinless, boneless chicken breasts, halved and flattened
Vegetable oil
Coarse salt
1/2 cup chicken stock
12 baby carrots, trimmed (reserve carrot tops for garnish)
1 cup sliced sweet onions
2 tablespoons honey
2 tablespoons freshly squeezed lemon juice
1/2 cup California dates, chopped
3 cups cooked rice
1/2 cup slivered toasted almonds, for garnish

Mix the spices together. Dust the chicken with the ground spices. Spray lightly with vegetable oil. Sprinkle with coarse salt.

Bring the chicken stock, carrots, and onions to a boil in a heavy skillet. Lower heat and simmer for 5 minutes or until the vegetables are tender-crisp. Stir in honey, lemon juice, and dates. Simmer for 1 minute or until the mixture is hot.

Meanwhile, grill the chicken over medium heat for 5 minutes per side until cooked through. Remove from the heat and slice the chicken on the bias into thin strips.

Arrange the sliced chicken, date mixture, and sauce over the hot rice on a platter or individual serving plates. Sprinkle with the slivered almonds and garnish with green carrot tops.

CALIFORNIA DATE DRESSING

Riverside County Fair and National Datefest

Here's a delicious, lowfat dip for a fruit or vegetable platter. Use a moist date, like the Medjool variety, for this recipe.

Makes 8 servings (approximately 1 cup)

1/3 cup lowfat pineapple yogurt
1/3 cup vegetable oil
1/4 cup buttermilk
1/4 cup California dates
1 teaspoon frozen orange juice concentrate or grated orange or lemon peel

In the container of an electric blender, combine all ingredients. Blend until the dates are finely chopped, turning the motor off and scraping down sides as needed. Refrigerate in a covered container up to 1 week. Serve with fruit, shredded carrot, or cabbage salads, or use as a fresh fruit dip.

CARAMELIZED DATE AND APPLE TART

Riverside County Fair and National Datefest

This beautiful and tasty dessert is made like a tarte Tatin: apples and dates are placed on a caramel mixture and then covered with a single layer of piecrust. It's baked in the oven and flipped over for serving.

Makes 6 servings

6 tablespoons sugar
3 tablespoons butter
1 teaspoon lemon juice
1/2 teaspoon corn syrup
4 Granny Smith apples or other green baking apples
16 California dates
1 ready-made piecrust

Preheat the oven to 400 degrees F.

Combine sugar, butter, lemon juice, and corn syrup in a 10-inch ovenproof skillet over medium-high heat. Cook 4 to 5 minutes, stirring constantly, until golden caramel brown. Remove from heat. (Remember that the caramel will continue to darken even after it is removed from the heat, so don't let it get too dark.)

Peel, core, and quarter apples. Arrange the quarters, rounded side down, around the edge of the ovenproof skillet. Fill in the center with the remaining apples. Place a date between each apple piece. Use extra dates to fill in empty spaces.

Measure piecrust dough. Roll it out to 11 inches if it is not already that size. Arrange the piecrust dough over the apples, folding it slightly, if necessary, and pushing it down between the fruit and the sides of the pan.

Bake for 25 to 30 minutes, or until the crust is golden brown. Remove from the oven and allow to cool several minutes. Invert onto a serving plate, slice, and serve.

CIOPPINO

48th Annual Precious Cheese North Beach Festival

Born in San Francisco's North Beach neighborhood (its "Little Italy"), this is probably the city's most famous dish. It's a "fisherman's stew" made by San Francisco's early inhabitants who used surpluses of their local catch. Thank you to chef Reed Hearon and Peggy Knickerbocker who provided us with their delicious, authentic recipe.

Makes 4 servings

1 live Dungeness crab (2 to 2 1/2 pounds)
1/4 cup extra virgin olive oil plus extra for drizzling
1 white onion, chopped
1/2 cup thinly sliced leeks (white part only)
2 garlic cloves, crushed
4 sprigs marjoram
6 anchovy fillets or 2 tablespoons anchovy paste
1/3 cup chopped flat-leaf parsley
1 teaspoon harissa or 1/2 teaspoon crushed red pepper flakes
1/2 pound lingcod or other white fish fillets, cut into small pieces
1 cup dry Italian white wine
1 cup pasta water or tap water
1 3/4 cups tomato purée (made from processing drained canned peeled whole tomatoes or peeled fresh whole tomatoes)
1/2 pound mussels, scrubbed and debearded
1/2 pound prawns or large shrimp, peeled and deveined
1/2 pound calamari, cleaned and cut into rings and tentacles
Kosher or sea salt to taste

Kill, clean, and section the crab as directed below, reserving the crab fat.

Warm the olive oil in a large heavy nonreactive pot over medium-high heat. Add the onions, leeks, and garlic, and sauté until the garlic is golden. Add the marjoram, anchovies, parsley, and harissa and stir to mix, mashing the anchovies with the tines of a fork. Add the crab and the fish and cook until the fish begins to fall apart, 7 to 10 minutes. Add the white wine and reduce by a third.

.   Mix the reserved crab fat, the pasta water or tap water, and tomato purée in a small bowl. Add this to the pot, raise the heat to high, and bring to a boil. Add the mussels and prawns and continue to boil until the mussel shells begin to open and the shrimp turns pink, about 3 minutes. Add the calamari and cook until stiffened, about 1 minute. Season with salt. Stir well. Ladle into a soup tureen and drizzle olive oil over the top. Serve at once with grilled bread.

Preparing Dungeness Crab for Cooking

It is always best to buy live crabs for the finest flavor and texture. You also are assured that the crab is fresh. For some recipes, the crabs are killed by immersing them in boiling water. They are then cleaned and sectioned. For others, they are killed and then cleaned and sectioned before cooking, as described here. If you kill the crab by immersion, skip to Step 4 for cleaning and cracking only.

1. Refrigerate the live crab until you're ready to cook it.
2. Wearing heavy gloves, if you wish, pick up the crab from behind to avoid being pinched. Grab all four legs and the claws on each side and hold them close to the body.
3. To kill the crab, using the edge of a heavy cutting board or the sink, crack the underside of the crab shell down the middle with one sharp blow. Alternatively, quickly puncture the area between the eyes with a sharp knife or ice pick.
4. With one hand, gather both sets of legs together. Grasp the back shell with the other hand and pull the back shell off. A lot of whitish or yellowish fat, also known as crab butter, will be visible in the back shell. Remove it and any additional fat hiding in the corners of the shell and set aside for later use.
5. Remove and discard the mouth parts, gills, and intestine.
6. Split the crab lengthwise through the body and cut each half into sections, with a leg attached to each section.
7. To crack the crab, after it has been cooked lay a clean kitchen towel over the crab pieces to avoid spattering and strike each leg and claw with a hammer or mallet.

SPAGHETTI WITH CALAMARI MEATBALLS

48th Annual Precious Cheese North Beach Festival

This is another dish that hails from San Francisco's North Beach district where the spirit of Italian cooking reigns supreme. It comes from *The Rose Pistola Cookbook* (Broadway Books, 1999) by chef Reed Hearon and Peggy Knickerbocker.

Makes 6 servings

1/4 cup plus 1 tablespoon extra virgin olive oil (more if needed)
1 1/2 white onions, chopped
2 garlic cloves, bruised
2 sprigs marjoram
1/2 cup chopped flat-leaf parsley
1 tablespoon plus 1 teaspoon harissa
14 anchovy fillets
1 pound calamari, cleaned and cut into rings and tentacles
1/4 pound pancetta, cut into small cubes
1 large egg white
1/2 cup bread crumbs
3/4 teaspoon kosher or sea salt, or more to taste
1 cup dry Italian white wine
1 cup tomato purée (made from processing drained canned peeled whole tomatoes or peeled fresh whole tomatoes)
2 tablespoons calamari ink
1 cup pasta water or tap water
1 pound spaghetti

Heat 1 tablespoon of the olive oil in a heavy skillet over medium-high heat. Add two-thirds of the onions, 1 garlic clove, 1 marjoram sprig, 1/4 cup of the parsley, 1 tablespoon of the harissa, and 10 of the anchovy fillets and sauté until the onion becomes translucent. Let cool. Remove the marjoram sprig.

Pulse all the calamari and pancetta, in small batches, in a food processor, keeping the mixture coarse, not smooth. Add the egg white and pulse to mix. Place the mixture in a bowl and stir in the bread crumbs, salt, and the cooled onion mixture. Form into golf ball–sized balls (using two soupspoons works well).

Heat 2 tablespoons of the olive oil in a large heavy skillet over medium-high heat and brown the calamari balls on all sides, adding more olive oil if needed. (You do not need to cook them all the way through, as they will finish cooking in the sauce.) Drain on paper towels.

Heat the remaining 2 tablespoons olive oil in a large, heavy sauté pan over medium-high heat. Add the remaining onions, garlic clove, marjoram sprig, $1/4$ cup parsley, 1 teaspoon harissa, and 4 anchovy fillets, and sauté until the onion becomes translucent. Add the wine and cook until reduced by half. Add the tomato purée and stir well. Dilute the calamari ink with the pasta water and stir it into the sauce. Add the calamari balls and simmer for about 30 minutes. Taste for seasoning. This can be done ahead of time to this point.

Meanwhile, bring a large pot of salted water to a boil. Cook the spaghetti 10 to 12 minutes or until al dente. Drain.

Bring the sauce back to a simmer. Add the spaghetti, stir well, and simmer over medium-high heat in the sauce until the sauce has reduced enough to coat the pasta, about 2 more minutes. Evenly distribute the pasta and calamari balls among 6 warm pasta bowls. Serve immediately.

PRECIOUS
Cheese
NORTH BEACH
Festival
GRANT
STOP

Welcome
Utica Old Fashioned
ICE CREAM FESTIVAL
6
7

SESAME BANANA NUT CRUNCH

Utica Old-Fashioned Ice Cream Festival

This deluxe banana split is probably one of the most creative you will ever find. It comes from Nancy Collins of Columbus, Ohio.

Makes 4 servings

4 medium bananas
1/4 cup (1/2 stick) butter or margarine
1/4 cup firmly packed brown sugar

Topping
1 (12 1/4-ounce) jar caramel ice cream topping
1 cup walnut pieces
1/4 cup sesame seeds
1 cup dried banana chips, crushed into pieces

1 quart Velvet Vanilla Lovers Trio ice cream

Slice the bananas lengthwise and then in half, dividing each banana into 4 pieces. In a large skillet, melt the butter. Warm bananas in butter, being careful not to break the banana pieces. Stir in the brown sugar and continue to heat until the sugar is caramelized.

In a microwave-safe bowl, in a microwave oven warm caramel sauce on Medium for 1 to 2 minutes, or until warm. Place 2 scoops of ice cream in each bowl and top with 4 pieces of fried banana. Divide caramel sauce, walnuts, sesame seeds, and banana chips over each bowl of ice cream.

STRAWBERRY ICE CREAM, PHILADELPHIA STYLE

Utica Old-Fashioned Ice Cream Festival

This is a delicious recipe from Bruce Weinstein's book *The Ultimate Ice Cream Cookbook* (William Morrow & Co., 1999). "Philadelphia style" ice creams are easy as they do not require a custard base.

Makes about 1 quart

2 cups heavy cream
1/3 cup sugar
3 cups fresh strawberries
1/4 cup milk

Heat the cream in a large saucepan over medium heat until small bubbles appear around the edge. Do not let the cream boil. Remove from the heat and add the sugar, stirring until the sugar dissolves completely. Cool to room temperature.

Meanwhile, cut the berries into quarters and place in a blender with the milk. Blend until the berries are puréed. Add the purée to the cooled cream. Refrigerate until cold or overnight. Freeze in l or 2 batches in your ice cream machine according to the manufacturer's instructions. When finished, the ice cream will be soft but ready to eat. For firmer ice cream, transfer to a freezer-safe container and freeze at least 2 hours.

Variation: Strawberry Banana Ice Cream

Thinly slice 2 small bananas and toss with 2 tablespoons sugar and 1 tablespoon banana liqueur or water. Allow the fruit to macerate for 1 hour. Combine the banana mixture with the cream before freezing. Proceed with the recipe as directed.

VELVET CRUNCH CAKE

Utica Old-Fashioned Ice Cream Festival

This ice-cream cake by Wilma Griffin of Westerville, Ohio, is a prize-winning recipe from the Utica Old-Fashioned Ice Cream Festival. It uses a Rice Krispy Treat–like mixture (made with chocolate and peanut butter instead of marshmallows) that is blended with ice cream. Kids and adults will love it.

Makes 12 servings

1 (1/2-ounce) package semisweet chocolate chips
2/3 cup smooth peanut butter
6 cups crispy rice cereal
1 gallon Velvet Olde Tyme Vanilla ice cream
Strawberries or raspberries, for garnish

In a large saucepan on low heat, melt the chocolate chips and peanut butter; add the cereal and stir to mix well. Spread on a waxed paper–lined cookie sheet and cool about 2 hours; break up cereal mixture in small pieces. Mixture will still be moist. Soften ice cream; fold in all but 1 1/2 cups of cereal mixture and spread in a 10-inch springform pan. Sprinkle the remaining cereal mixture over the top and freeze. Garnish with strawberries or raspberries.

HERMIS
FALKNER
PENA
ROBERTS

GOLDEN TILAPIA

U.S. Army Culinary Classic

This recipe won a gold medal at the annual U.S. Army Culinary competition, where it was served with Asian Rice Cakes (page 91) and Szechuan Mixed Vegetables (page 90). The marinade gives the fish a golden brown color and highly appealing taste.

Makes 4 servings

1/3 teaspoon peppercorns and 1 clove, toasted over medium heat in a dry skillet for 1 minute and crushed
2 teaspoons sugar
3 tablespoons soy sauce
2 tablespoons white rum
1/2 teaspoon grated lemon peel
1 tablespoon lemon juice
Salt and pepper
1 teaspoon ground ginger
1 teaspoon garlic powder
1 pound tilapia fillets
Oil
Szechuan Mixed Vegetables

Place the sugar, soy sauce, rum, lemon peel, and lemon juice in a small saucepan. Add all of the spices, and over medium heat, reduce by half. Remove from the heat, strain, and let cool. Place the fillets in the marinade and marinate for 20 minutes.

Preheat the oven to 375 degrees F. In a skillet on medium-high heat, add a small amount of oil and sauté the fillets for 2 minutes on each side. Place 4 piles (1/3 cup each) of the Szechuan Mixed Vegetables on a baking sheet, place the fillets on top and finish cooking in the oven for 5 to 7 minutes or until done.

While the fish is cooking, bring the reserved marinade to boil in a skillet over high heat. Lower the heat and reduce the marinade until thick, about 2 minutes.

Remove the fish from the oven and brush with the reduced marinade. Serve immediately.

SZECHUAN MIXED VEGETABLES

U.S. Army Culinary Classic

Here's a colorful vegetable dish with an Asian twist. If you've never learned the proper way to julienne a vegetable, take the time to learn and be sure to practice. The julienne cut gives simple food a very attractive appearance.

Makes 4 servings

Vegetable oil cooking spray
1/4 cup julienned carrots
1/4 cup julienned celery
1/4 cup julienned red bell pepper
1/4 cup julienned yellow bell pepper
1/2 teaspoon minced fresh garlic
1 teaspoon crushed red pepper flakes
2 tablespoons water
Salt and freshly ground pepper to taste
2 tablespoons toasted peanuts, for garnish

Spray a skillet with oil. Add the vegetables, garlic, and crushed red pepper flakes and sauté, tossing frequently for about 3 minutes, until half cooked. Add the water and steam the vegetables until they are tender, about 4 minutes. Season with salt and pepper. Garnish with the toasted peanuts and serve immediately.

ASIAN RICE CAKES

U.S. Army Culinary Classic

This is a wonderful healthy side dish that can accompany many main courses. Short-grain rice, after it's cooked and cooled, becomes sticky enough to form a ball. When the cakes are browned, the result is a crunchy coating with a creamy, soft inside that's flavored with ginger and green onion.

Makes 4 servings

1/2 cup short-grain rice
1 cup water
2 teaspoons rice wine vinegar
2 tablespoons thinly sliced green onions
1 tablespoon pickled ginger root, chopped
Vegetable oil cooking spray

Place the rice and water in a small saucepan, cover, and cook 20 minutes, stirring occasionally. When rice is cooked, add the remaining ingredients. Let cook slightly and shape into desired shapes.

In a well-heated nonstick skillet sprayed with oil, place the rice cakes and brown on both sides until golden brown. Place on a baking sheet and keep warm in the oven until ready to serve.

ROAST PORK TENDERLOINS WITH CRANBERRY-BURGUNDY WINE SAUCE

U.S. Army Culinary Classic

Here's another prizewinning recipe found at the U.S. Army culinary arts competition in the Pork Category. Pork tenderloin, with a lower fat content than many meats, is dressed up here with a colorful and delightful cranberry sauce. Cranberries can be difficult to find outside of the fall season, so you may want to keep some on hand in your freezer.

Makes 2 servings

1 tablespoon butter
3/4 cup chopped onions
1 clove garlic, minced
1 tablespoon grated orange peel
1/2 teaspoon dried sage
2 1/2 teaspoons dried thyme
1 cup low-salt chicken broth
1 cup cranberry juice
3/4 cup cranberries, fresh or frozen and thawed
1/4 cup sugar
2 tablespoons Burgundy cooking wine
1 tablespoon cornstarch
1 1/2 teaspoons salt plus more to taste
1/2 teaspoon freshly ground black pepper plus more to taste
1 (6-ounce) pork tenderloin, trimmed of excess fat
2 tablespoons vegetable oil

Melt butter in a heavy large skillet over medium-high heat. Add onions and sauté until golden, about 8 minutes. Add garlic, 1 1/2 teaspoons orange peel, sage, and 1 teaspoon thyme; stir for 1 minute. Add the chicken broth and cranberry juice; simmer until mixture is reduced to 2 1/2 cups, about 8 minutes. Strain the sauce into a heavy medium saucepan, pressing solids with the back of the spoon. Add cranberries and sugar; boil

just until cranberries pop, about 5 minutes. Mix Burgundy cooking wine and cornstarch in a small bowl to blend. Add to the sauce; boil until the sauce thickens, about 1 minute. Season with salt and pepper. (Cranberry sauce can be made 1 day ahead. Cover and refrigerate.)

Mix remaining $1\frac{1}{2}$ teaspoons thyme, $1\frac{1}{2}$ teaspoons salt, and $\frac{1}{2}$ teaspoon pepper in a small bowl. Place pork in a large baking dish. Pat dry with a paper towel. Brush with 1 tablespoon oil. Rub thyme mixture over pork. (Can be prepared 1 day ahead. Cover and refrigerate.)

Preheat oven to 400 degrees F. Heat remaining 1 tablespoon oil in a heavy large ovenproof skillet over high heat. Add pork and cook until brown, turning frequently, about 5 minutes. Transfer skillet to the oven and roast pork until the internal temperature at the thickest part of the pork reaches 150 degrees F, about 20 minutes. Transfer pork to platter; cover to keep warm. Add cranberry sauce and remaining $1\frac{1}{2}$ teaspoons orange peel to the same skillet and bring to a simmer, stirring frequently.

Slice pork into diagonal slices. Sauce plates and divide slices between 2 plates.

GARLIC MASHED POTATOES WITH MASCARPONE

U.S. Army Culinary Classic

Chives and mascarpone cheese add a wonderful rich flavor to these mashed potatoes. You can substitute sour cream if you wish.

Makes 2 servings

1 1/4 russet potatoes
2 tablespoons half and half
Salt and freshly ground black pepper to taste
2 cloves garlic, roasted
2 tablespoons butter
1/4 cup mascarpone cheese
2 tablespoons grated Parmesan cheese
2 tablespoons chopped chives

Peel and wash potatoes, place in boiling salted water, and cook until tender. Drain; place in the bowl of an electric stand mixer. Add half and half, salt, pepper, garlic, butter, cheeses, and chives. Whip until smooth. Serve immediately.

GREEN BEANS WITH BALSAMIC-SHALLOT BUTTER

U.S. Army Culinary Classic

Here's an interesting way to perk up green beans with a special butter that's flavored with shallots and a balsamic reduction. The butter can be made a day ahead, making this a quick dish to put together for a dinner party.

Makes 2 servings

1/4 cup balsamic vinegar
2 large shallots, finely chopped
1 tablespoon butter, at room temperature
20 green beans, trimmed
Salt and freshly ground black pepper to taste

Combine vinegar and shallots in a heavy small saucepan. Boil over medium heat, stirring frequently, until most of the vinegar is absorbed (about 1 tablespoon liquid should remain in the pan), about 6 minutes. Transfer mixture to a small bowl; cool completely. Add butter and mix with a fork until blended.

Cook the beans in a large pot of boiling salted water until crisp-tender, about 6 minutes. Drain. Refresh under cold water; drain again. Pat dry with paper towels. (Balsamic-shallot butter and beans can be made 1 day ahead. Cover separately; chill.)

Combine beans and balsamic-shallot butter in a large nonstick skillet. Toss over medium heat until the beans are heated through, about 5 minutes. Season with salt and pepper and serve.

NET WT 20Kg
SUN BRAND

NASI GORENG (FRIED RICE)

Singapore Food Festival

Nasi Goreng literally translated from Indonesian means "fried rice." Versions of this dish are found in all corners of Asia. This particular recipe is infused with a pungent paste of garlic and anchovies, creating a flavorful accompaniment to almost any meal. This recipe comes from **at-sunrice,** Singapore's premier culinary school.

Makes 4 servings

6 cups boiled rice
8 shallots
4 fresh red chiles
3 cloves garlic, peeled
2 1/2 ounces ikan bilis (anchovy)
3 tablespoons oil, for frying
2 eggs
1 tablespoon light soy sauce
Salt to taste
1 cup fried shallots
4 eggs, fried

Stir rice with a fork to make sure grains are separated.

In a blender or food processor, blend shallots, chiles, garlic, and ikan bilis into a fine paste. Heat the oil in a wok and fry the paste over medium heat, stirring constantly, about 8 minutes until fragrant. Add the eggs and stir-fry over high heat for 2 minutes. Remove from the wok.

Add the rice and soy sauce to the wok; stir-fry and mix well. Season with salt.

Garnish the rice with the fried shallots and egg and serve hot.

CHICKEN RENDANG (RICH COCONUT CHICKEN STEW)

Singapore Food Festival

Kaffir lime leaves, found in most Asian markets, are an important ingredient in Southeast Asian cooking. The leaves, along with the lemongrass stalks, impart a wonderful citrus flavor to this sumptuous coconut stew, another wonderful recipe provided by **at-sunrice: The Singapore Cooking School and Spice Garden.**

Makes 4 servings

8 dry medium red chiles, softened in boiling water for 5 minutes and drained
10 small shallots, finely chopped
7 cloves garlic, finely chopped
1/4 cup (2 ounces) finely chopped ginger
2 tablespoons cooking oil
2 tablespoons (1 ounce) peeled and thinly sliced galangal (Thai ginger)
2 stalks lemongrass, smashed
5 kaffir lime leaves, torn
1 turmeric leaf
1 whole chicken (about 2 pounds), cut into 8 pieces
1 1/2 cups coconut milk
1 tablespoon salt or to taste
Palm sugar or brown sugar to taste
Fried shallots, for garnish (optional)

In a blender or food processor, grind the softened dry chiles, shallots, garlic, and ginger into a fine paste.

Heat the oil in a stew pot over medium heat and fry the paste for 10 minutes, until fragrant. Be careful not to burn the paste. Keep adding some oil a little at a time if the paste becomes too dry.

Add the galangal, lemongrass, kaffir lime leaves, turmeric leaf, and chicken pieces. Stir in the coconut milk and add salt to taste. Bring to a simmer (never boil), cover, and stir from time to time, until the chicken is cooked, about 20 minutes.

Add the palm sugar, increase the heat to medium-high, and cook a few more minutes, until the sauce has thickened.

Serve hot with steamed or turmeric rice, topped with fried shallots if you desire.

Note: Rendang is very good for barbequed meat. Marinate the meat in the paste mixed with a little oil for at least 30 minutes. Then proceed to grill as desired.

ACHAR

Singapore Food Festival

This refreshing relish proves that Singapore is the "Culinary Crossroads of the Pacific." Originating in East India, this simple dish is often served as a cooling condiment to the fiery flavors found all over Singapore.

Makes 4 servings

3 carrots, julienned
4 cucumbers, julienned
1 pineapple, sliced
1 galangal (Thai ginger)
6 to 7 red chiles, seeded
15 shallots
2 candle nuts, macadamia nuts, or walnuts
1 cup white vinegar
1½ cups sugar
1 teaspoon salt

In a large mixing bowl, add carrots, cucumber, and pineapple and stir to combine. In a blender or food processor, grind galangal, chiles, shallots, and candle nuts with a little water.

In a small saucepan, heat the ground ingredients to bring out the flavor and add to the vegetables. Add the vinegar, sugar, and salt and mix all ingredients well. Refrigerate for 2 minutes to allow the flavors to meld together. Serve cold or at room temperature.

MANGO LASSI (INDIAN DRINK)

Singapore Food Festival

This delightful beverage calls for cardamom, which is one of the oldest spices in the world. It is a member of the ginger family and lends a sweet, peppery zest to this soothing recipe.

Makes 4 servings

1 large mango, peeled and cut from the pit
1 cup plain lowfat yogurt
1 teaspoon sugar
$^1/_4$ teaspoon cardamom
$2^1/_2$ cups ice cubes

Place all ingredients in a blender and beat until smooth. Serve cold.

BANANA FRITTERS

Singapore Food Festival

This unique recipe relies on eggs as the only leavening agent. The result is a dense, moist fritter that needs very little embellishing. Be sure to heat the oil to the proper temperature before frying, to guarantee a crisp, golden crust.

Makes 2 servings

4 eggs
3/4 cup flour
1/2 cup water
4 ripe bananas
Oil for deep frying
Cinnamon sugar to taste

Slightly beat the eggs and mix with the flour and water. Mash the bananas with a fork and mix thoroughly into the egg and flour mixture.

Deep-fry banana and flour mixture by the tablespoonful in hot oil until golden brown. Drain on paper towels and dust with cinnamon sugar.

BEEF SATAY

Singapore Food Festival

The streets of Singapore are infused with the aromas of this popular dish. "Hawker stalls" or outdoor eateries often boast the "Best Satay in Asia." Galangal (also known as blue ginger) is a key ingredient in this version. It looks very similar to its relative, the common yellow ginger, but has a distinct sour essence.

Makes 4 servings

Spice Paste

3 1/2 tablespoons (1 3/4 ounces) chopped lemongrass
2 tablespoons (1 ounce) minced garlic
1 teaspoon turmeric
1 tablespoon coriander
1 teaspoon cumin
1 teaspoon salt
1 teaspoon sugar

1 1/4 pounds (600g) beef, cut into long strips
1 stalk lemongrass, lightly bruised to form a brush
Oil

Satay Sauce

6 to 8 dried chiles, soaked in hot water till soft
6 cloves garlic
3 shallots
4 stalks lemongrass
1 (1-inch) piece galangal
2 tablespoons ground coriander
2 tablespoons ground cumin

1 tablespoon vegetable oil
1/3 cup tamarind pulp, soaked in 1 tablespoon water
1 cup sugar
1 tablespoon salt or to taste
2 cups dry-roasted peanuts, coarsely crushed

Blend the Spice Paste ingredients together in a blender or food processor until fine. Spread the paste over the beef and marinate for 3 to 4 hours.

Thread 4 or 5 pieces of meat onto a bamboo skewer. Grill over a charcoal fire, constantly brushing with crushed lemongrass dipped in oil. Turn frequently to prevent burning. The meat should be slightly blackened on the outside and just cooked inside.

To make the sauce: Chop the dried chiles, garlic, shallots, lemongrass, galangal, coriander, and cumin in a blender or food processor into a fine paste. Heat the oil and fry the paste together with the tamarind pulp, until fragrant, adding the water a little at a time. Add sugar, salt, and peanuts. Mix thoroughly and set aside. Serve at room temperature with satay.

PEAR BERRY CRUSH

Courtland Pear Fair

This fruit smoothie, which combines the unbeatable combination of strawberry and pears, is a refreshing drink. Remember that green, hard pears purchased in a supermarket need to be ripened for several days at home until they turn yellow and fragrant.

Makes 2 servings

1 (10-ounce) package frozen strawberries
2 Bartlett pears, cored and coarsely chopped
12 ice cubes

Place ingredients in a blender and whirl until smooth. Pour into 2 tall glasses and serve immediately.

FRUITY SALSA

Courtland Pear Fair

This is a quick recipe for those times when you'd like a refreshing salsa but can't spend a lot of time chopping lots of fruits and vegetables. It's great with grilled meats and seafood.

Makes about 4 cups

2 Bartlett pears, chopped
1 cup diced cantaloupe, in 1/4-inch cubes
1 1/2 cups mild salsa

Combine ingredients and use as an accompaniment to grilled seafood or chicken.

CREAMY FRUIT DIP

Courtland Pear Fair

This is a great item to serve with a fruit plate for a brunch or afternoon snack. Try serving with skewers of strawberries and pineapple or any of your favorite fruits. Don't be afraid to substitute canned pears, which generally contain high-quality pears.

Makes 1 cup

2 fresh California Bartlett pears, cored
1/4 cup plain lowfat yogurt
1 (3-ounce) package cream cheese
1 teaspoon grated fresh ginger or fresh lemon or lime peel

In a blender, combine all of the ingredients except the ginger. Blend until smooth. Add the ginger and blend to mix. Pour into a serving dish and serve with fresh pear wedges.

PEAR SAUCE

Courtland Pear Fair

This is an excellent sauce to serve over ice cream, pancakes, or waffles—or anything that could use an extra layer of sweet fruit flavor.

Makes 1 3/4 cups

2 tablespoons sugar
1 teaspoon cornstarch
1/2 cup water
1 strip lemon peel
1 tablespoon lemon juice
Pinch salt
2 Bartlett pears, diced

In a medium saucepan, combine the sugar and cornstarch; add the water, lemon peel, lemon juice, and salt. Cook and stir over medium-high heat until thickened. Gently stir in diced pears. Remove from the heat. Serve immediately over cheesecake, fresh fruit, pancakes, ice cream, or waffles.

PEAR CHUTNEY

Courtland Pear Fair

Chutneys are excellent accompaniments to grilled meats like pork or chicken. They can be made the day before and store well in the refrigerator.

Makes 6 servings

3 ripe but firm California Bartlett pears, peeled, cored, and chopped
1 onion, chopped
1/4 cup red wine vinegar
1/4 cup firmly packed brown sugar
1 tablespoon finely grated orange peel
1 tablespoon finely grated ginger
1/4 teaspoon allspice
1 clove garlic
2 tablespoons dried cranberries

Combine all of the ingredients except the cranberries in a medium saucepan; stir well to combine. Cover and simmer for 55 minutes over very low heat. Stir in the cranberries and cook for 5 minutes more. Let cool to room temperature before serving.

ZINFANDEL BRAISED LAMB SHANKS WITH WHITE BEANS AND BACON

Lambtown USA

Lamb shanks are extremely popular among chefs who love how they cook down into a tender meat, soaked in the flavors of their favorite braising liquid. The braising liquid in this recipe contains zinfandel and tomatoes; after hours of cooking with the lamb, it makes a wonderful, natural sauce for the meat.

Makes 4 servings

4 (1-pound) lamb shanks, well trimmed
2 tablespoons olive oil
2 yellow onions, chopped
1 carrot, chopped
1 stalk celery, chopped
6 cloves garlic, minced
1 tablespoon chopped fresh rosemary
4 cups red zinfandel wine
4 cups chicken broth
1 (14-ounce) can crushed tomatoes
4 strips bacon
5 cups cooked or canned small white beans
Salt and pepper to taste

Preheat oven to 350 degrees F.

In a heavy skillet, brown the lamb shanks on all sides in olive oil; remove to an ovenproof casserole and set aside. Add 1 chopped onion, the chopped carrot, and chopped celery to the same skillet and brown. Stir in garlic and rosemary. Cook for 2 minutes. Add the wine, chicken broth, and crushed tomatoes and heat to boiling. Spoon the mixture over the lamb shanks and bake for 2 hours, or until the internal temperature of the thickest part reaches 155 degrees F.

Meanwhile, fry the bacon until crisp. Drain, crumble, and set aside. Remove excess fat from the pan and add remaining chopped onion to the same pan. Stir in the white beans and heat through. Stir in crumbled bacon, salt, and pepper. Spoon the bean mixture onto a platter or individual plates. Arrange the lamb shanks on top. Skim the fat from the vegetable mixture left in the casserole and spoon over all. Serve immediately.

SIMPLY GLAZED LEG OF LAMB

Lambtown USA

This may be simple, but it's quite special, with a finishing glaze that is one of the best we've ever tried. Leg of lamb can be found boneless, bone-in, or with partial bone-in; either way, the recipe works. Just keep checking the internal meat temperature for doneness.

Makes 6 to 8 servings

1 (5- to 7-pound) leg of fresh California lamb
2 cloves garlic, cut into slivers
1/2 teaspoon dry mustard
1/2 teaspoon finely minced fresh ginger, or 1/4 teaspoon ground ginger
1/2 teaspoon salt
1/2 teaspoon freshly ground black pepper
1/3 cup tart red jelly
1/2 teaspoon grated lemon peel
1 tablespoon lemon juice

Preheat oven to 325 degrees F.

Cut several slits in the leg of lamb and insert garlic slivers. Place lamb on a rack in a shallow baking pan and place in the oven. Cook 15 to 20 minutes per pound.

Meanwhile, in a small saucepan stir together the dry mustard, ginger, salt, and pepper. Add the jelly, lemon peel, and lemon juice. Cook over low heat until the jelly is melted and the seasonings are well blended.

Approximately 30 minutes before the lamb is done, or when the internal temperature reaches 130 degrees F, remove from the oven and brush with the jelly glaze. Return the lamb to the oven and cook 30 minutes, or until the internal temperature is 140 degrees F. Brush once or twice with jelly glaze during this time.

Remove the lamb from the oven, cover, and let stand for 15 minutes before slicing and serving. Final internal temperature for medium-rare is 145 to 150 degrees F and 160 degrees F for medium. Discard unused glaze.

SHANDONG LAMB

Lambtown USA

This recipe, submitted by Jack H. Su, won first prize at the Lambtown USA cook-off in Dixon, California, where the competition was steep. If you can't find Chinese mushrooms in your area, substitute a mushroom of your choice.

Makes 6 servings

Marinade

$1^{7}/_{8}$ cups (15 ounces) oyster sauce
$1^{1}/_{4}$ cups soy sauce
$1^{1}/_{4}$ teaspoons salt
$^{1}/_{2}$ cup cooking wine
2 tablespoons freshly ground white pepper

2 pounds lamb
1 pound onions
2 pounds Chinese black mushrooms
1 pound green bell peppers
1 tablespoon vegetable oil
$^{1}/_{4}$ teaspoon cayenne pepper
$^{1}/_{4}$ teaspoon Indian cumin

In a shallow bowl or baking dish, mix the marinade ingredients. Cut the lamb into cubes, place in the marinade in the refrigerator, and marinate for 1 hour.

Cut the onions, mushrooms, and bell peppers into cubes. Alternately thread mushrooms, onions, peppers, and lamb cubes on skewers. Lightly brush the skewers with the vegetable oil. Season with the cayenne and cumin. Grill the skewers over medium heat for 10 minutes.

Remove the skewers from the grill, place on individual plates, and serve with red potatoes.

Reynolds Wrap
Release
NON-STICK
Release
NON-STICK

WILLKOMMEN ZUM
OKTOBERFEST
WC

BEEF ROULADES

Oktoberfest

This traditional German dish comes from Master Chef Karl Guggenmos and consists of sliced beef rolled around a bacon-onion-pickle filling. It's a real treat and makes a wonderful main course for company. Have your butcher preslice the meat since it needs to be quite thin before rolled.

Makes 12 servings

1/3 cup butter, melted
2 cups diced onion
1 pound bacon, cooked and chopped
Salt, freshly ground black pepper, and paprika
12 (8-ounce) slices top round
Mustard
Ketchup
1 cup julienned pickles
1 tablespoon vegetable oil
1/2 cup chopped carrots
1/2 cup chopped celery
1 teaspoon tomato paste
2 tablespoons flour
1/4 cup dry red wine
6 cups beef broth
Salt and freshly ground black pepper to taste
2 cups heavy cream (optional)

Preheat oven to 400 degrees F.

Heat 1 tablespoon of the melted butter in a medium skillet over medium-high heat. When hot, add 1 cup diced onion and the cooked bacon. Season with salt and pepper. Cook the onions and bacon until tender, about 6 minutes. Transfer this mixture to a dinner plate and refrigerate until cold.

On a clean, flat work surface, lay out the meat slices. With a meat mallet, flatten the slices until about 1/4 inch thick. Season the meat with salt, pepper, and paprika. Smear the slices with mustard and ketchup. Place an equal amount of the pickles, bacon, and onions on the meat slices. Roll the slices up to form roulades. Tie with kitchen string or secure with large toothpicks. Place the roulades in a roasting pan. Coat the roulades with the remaining melted butter.

Oven-sear the roulades for 30 minutes or until evenly browned.

While the roulades are in the oven, heat the oil in a large skillet. Add the remaining 1 cup diced onion, carrots, and celery. Sauté until tender, about 15 minutes. Add the tomato paste. Cook for 1 minute. Add the flour and stir until well blended. Add the wine, stirring well and scraping the browned bits from the bottom of the pan. Add the broth and bring to a boil. Pour this braising sauce into the pan containing the roulades. Cover the roasting pan and return to the 400-degree oven. Braise for about 2 hours, turning the roulades occasionally.

Remove the pan from the oven. Transfer the roulades to a warm serving platter. Remove the kitchen string or toothpick from each roulade. Cover and keep warm.

Strain the sauce into a saucepan. Bring to a boil over high heat. Reduce the heat to low. Simmer until the sauce thickens. Season with salt and pepper. If desired, heavy cream may be added to this sauce during the last 5 minutes of simmering.

Pour the sauce over the roulades and serve immediately.

KARTOFFEL SUPPE (BAVARIAN POTATO SOUP)

Oktoberfest

If soups have somehow dropped from your radar, we'd recommend corralling them back in—and it won't be hard with this delicious, flavorful, and satisfying potato soup.

Makes 12 servings

1/2 pound bacon, diced
1/2 carrot, diced
1 stalk celery, diced
1/2 small leek, sliced
1 onion, diced
3 large new potatoes, diced
1/2 bunch parsley, chopped
1/4 teaspoon chopped marjoram
1/4 cup all-purpose flour
1 1/2 quarts beef stock
Salt, garlic, black pepper, and nutmeg

Render bacon in a stockpot. Add the vegetables, potatoes, and herbs. Sauté until transparent. Dust with flour. Add the stock and simmer for 30 to 40 minutes. Season to taste. Serve with freshly baked bread.

HB
MÜNCHEN

ROTKRAUT MIT APFELN (RED CABBAGE WITH APPLES)

Oktoberfest

This wonderful German side dish combines apples, cabbage, and onions with sweet and sour flavors, long-simmered together for a memorable, penetrating flavor. The vinegar added to the cabbage just after it's shredded allows it to keep its red color during cooking.

Makes 10 to 12 servings

1 pound red cabbage
1/3 cup red wine vinegar
1 teaspoon salt
1 tablespoon sugar
2 strips bacon
1 apple, peeled, cored, and cut into 1/8-inch wedges
1/4 cup finely chopped onions plus 1 onion, peeled and pierced with 2 cloves
1 bay leaf
1/2 cup boiling water
2 tablespoons dry red wine
1 1/2 tablespoons red currant jelly

Wash and shred the cabbage into 1/8-inch strips. In a mixing bowl, sprinkle the cabbage with vinegar, salt, and sugar. Toss until evenly coated. In a sauté pan, render the bacon. Add the apples and chopped onions to the pan and sauté until lightly brown. Add the cabbage, whole onion with cloves, bay leaf, and boiling water. Bring to a boil, and then lower heat to simmer. Add the wine and currant jelly. Cover and simmer for 1 1/2 hours or until cabbage is tender. Cabbage should be tender once all the liquid is gone. If needed, add 1 to 2 cups water and continue simmering. Remove the whole onion and bay leaf. Adjust seasoning and serve.

BAVARIAN POTATO SALAD

Oktoberfest

The oil—not mayonnaise—in this potato salad flavored with chicken stock, onions, and mustard is a refreshing and delicious change, especially for people trying to reduce cholesterol intake. It's best made with a low-starch potato, such as Yukon Gold or new potatoes.

Makes 4 servings

1 pound Yukon or California Gold potatoes
6 tablespoons chicken broth
3 tablespoons vinegar
1/4 cup finely chopped onions
Mustard, salt, pepper, and sugar to taste
1 to 2 tablespoons oil
1 tablespoon chopped chives or parsley
Crisp, crumbled bacon, for garnish (optional)
Cubed apples, for garnish (optional)

Boil unpeeled potatoes in salted water until tender. Drain and let dry for 20 minutes. Peel while warm and thinly slice. In a skillet, bring broth, vinegar, onions, mustard, salt, pepper, and sugar to a boil. Pour oil over potatoes and pour boiling hot marinade over the potatoes. Shake and toss for 2 minutes to loosen the starch. Adjust seasoning and add chives. Allow to rest for 30 minutes. Serve at room temperature. If desired, add crisp bacon or cubed apples.

weber

SPIT-ROASTED CHICKEN

Oktoberfest

You can see beautifully browned spit-roasted chickens, with their crispy skin and juicy meat, at the Oktoberfest in Munich as well as throughout most of Germany. The bonus to spit-roasting is that much of the chicken fat drips away during cooking.

Makes 4 servings

2 medium chickens
Salt and pepper
3 tablespoons oil

Season chicken with salt and pepper and truss. Spray with oil and roast on a spit or in a 350-degree oven for 40 minutes, or until the internal temperature is 170 degrees F. Allow to rest for 10 minutes, then split the chicken and remove the ribcage before serving.

OBATZTA (BAVARIAN CHEESE DISH)

Oktoberfest

Our dear friend, Master Chef Fritz Sonnenschmidt, provided us with recipes for a wonderful German meal, including this savory cheese appetizer, which can be made with any cheese that has a rind, such as Brie or Camembert.

Makes 4 servings

9 ounces Camembert
6 tablespoons soft butter
1 small onion, diced
Paprika, pepper, and salt to taste
2 tablespoons beer
1 tablespoon chopped chives
Sliced radishes, for garnish

Mash all ingredients with a fork. Arrange on Boston lettuce leaves. Garnish with radishes. Serve with pumpernickel and a stein of beer.

GINGER GLAZED CARROTS

Oktoberfest

This easy dish uses ginger to spice up carrots and makes an excellent side dish.

Makes 4 to 6 servings

1¹/₄ pounds carrots
¹/₄ cup (¹/₂ stick) butter
Lemon juice to taste
Ginger, salt, pepper, and sugar to taste
¹/₄ cup chicken stock

Use a sharp knife to cut the carrots into ¹/₄ by ¹/₄ by 2-inch sticks. Combine all of the ingredients in a medium skillet over high heat. Bring to a boil. Reduce the heat to a simmer and allow to cook, stirring occasionally, until the carrots are tender and the cooking liquid becomes thick and shiny, about 15 minutes. Serve the carrots immediately.

QUICK SOUR CREAM COFFEE CAKE

Oktoberfest

Streusel means "to sprinkle" in German. In this recipe, nuts and cinnamon are added to the traditional crumb topping of butter, flour, and sugar. Don't be shy in sprinkling this mixture on top of this foolproof cake.

Makes 6 servings

1 1/2 cups sifted flour
1 cup sugar
2 teaspoons baking powder
1/2 teaspoon baking soda
1/4 teaspoon salt
1 cup sour cream
2 eggs

Streusel
2 tablespoons flour
2 tablespoons butter
5 tablespoons sugar
1/2 teaspoon cinnamon
1/2 cup chopped nuts

Preheat the oven to 350 degrees F. Sift together the flour, sugar, baking powder, baking soda, and salt. In a mixing bowl, blend the sour cream and eggs. Add sifted ingredients to the cream mixture and beat just until smooth. Spread in a lightly greased pan.

To make the streusel: In a small mixing bowl, blend the flour, butter, and sugar together until they crumble. Add the cinnamon and chopped nuts.

Sprinkle the streusel over the cake mixture in the pan. Bake for about 20 minutes, until a toothpick inserted in the center comes out clean. Remove the cake from the oven and allow to rest at room temperature for 10 minutes in the baking pan. Turn the baking pan upside down to release the cake from the pan (you may need to tap the edge a little to facilitate removal). Turn the cake right side up and transfer to a cake rack to cool further at room temperature. Serve slightly warm with ice cream or whipped cream.

HOTEL
DEL RIO
CRAWDAD TOWN U.S.A.
SLETON
CRAWDAD FE

CRAWFISH BISQUE

Isleton Crawdad Festival

This has the elements of a traditional bisque: puréed seafood and cream. Unlike chicken stock, fish stocks are very quick to make. Use the crawfish shells for the stock or get shrimp or lobster shells from your seafood purveyor.

Makes 4 to 6 servings

1/2 cup finely diced onion
1 cup finely diced celery
1 cup finely diced carrot
3 1/2 tablespoons butter, softened
1 (15-ounce) can tomatoes, cut into pieces (use the juice for another dish)
5 cups shrimp stock or fish stock
1 cup dry white wine (dry vermouth is excellent)
2 tablespoons olive oil
1 pound crawfish meat
1/2 cup heavy cream
Salt and pepper to taste
1 tablespoon chopped fresh tarragon or other mild herb
Whole cooked crawfish and croutons, for garnish

In a large skillet or stockpot, sauté the onion, celery, and carrot (called a *mirepoix*) in 1 tablespoon of the butter for 5 minutes, until the vegetables are soft. Add the tomato pieces and sauté for another 5 minutes. Add stock and wine and cook for 15 minutes.

In a separate skillet, heat olive oil and 1/2 tablespoon butter. Sauté the crawfish meat for a couple of minutes and let cool.

When the soup has finished cooking, add it to a blender with half the crawfish meat and blend. Strain back into the pot.

Enrich the soup by whisking in the remaining 2 tablespoons of butter and the cream. Season with salt and pepper. Let sit for flavors to blend, until ready to serve.

Mince the tarragon finely. Ladle the soup into bowls, top with the cooked crawfish and minced herbs and garnish with croutons or thinly sliced toasted bread.

LINGUINE CRAWFISH TOSS

Isleton Crawdad Festival

This is a delicious sauce that comes together quickly. You can substitute lobster or shrimp meat for the crawfish.

Makes 6 to 8 servings

1 pound linguine
2 tablespoons butter
2 shallots, chopped
2 cloves garlic, minced
1/2 cup dry white wine
20 crawfish tails
1 cup frozen peas
1/2 cup dried tomatoes, cut into strips
Zest of 1 lemon
Salt and freshly ground black pepper to taste
2 tablespoons olive oil
3 tablespoons chopped parsley
6 lemon wedges, for garnish

Prepare the linguine according to the package directions. Melt the butter and cook the shallot and garlic in a large skillet. Add the white wine and simmer until reduced by half. Add crawfish and cook about 2 minutes. Add peas, tomatoes, lemon zest, salt, and pepper and warm through. Add oil and parsley to linguine and toss. Top the linguine with the crawfish mixture. Garnish with lemon wedges and serve.

CAJUN CRAWFISH ÉTOUFFÉE

Isleton Crawdad Festival

In Cajun cooking, *étouffée* means "smothered in a sauce." Here the crawfish and vegetables are smothered in a spicy sauce. You can substitute lobster or shrimp for crawfish.

Makes 4 servings

1 pound fresh or frozen peeled crawfish tails or shrimp
2 large onions, chopped (1 1/2 cups)
1 cup chopped celery
1 cup each chopped green and red bell pepper
1 tablespoon chopped garlic
1 tablespoon butter
1 cup water
1/2 cup tomato sauce
1/2 teaspoon salt
1/2 teaspoon paprika
2 to 3 dashes hot pepper sauce
2 bay leaves
1/4 to 1/2 teaspoon cayenne pepper
1/4 teaspoon freshly ground black pepper
1 cup brown roux
Cooked rice

Thaw crawfish or shrimp if frozen. In a heavy, 3-quart saucepan, cook onions, celery, green pepper, red pepper, and garlic in butter for about 10 minutes, or until tender. Stir in crawfish or shrimp, water, tomato sauce, and spices. Bring mixture to boiling. Add the brown roux and whisk until smooth. Reduce heat. Simmer, uncovered, about 5 minutes or until crawfish are tender or shrimp turn opaque. Serve with hot cooked rice.

Note: The orange fat inside crawfish heads is in the original recipe and adds a rich flavor. Crawfish fat can be hard to find, so we've substituted butter.

BLACK BEAN–ROASTED CORN SALSA

Festival de la Familia

This comes from New York City chef Rafael Palomino and his popular book, *Bistro Latino* (William Morrow & Co., 1998). The dish falls somewhere between a salsa and a salad and makes a great accompaniment to grilled fish, chicken, or meat. Try grilling the corn for extra flavor.

Makes about 4 cups

4 ears corn (do not remove the husks) or 2 cups frozen kernels
2 tablespoons olive oil
1 clove garlic, minced
2 cups drained freshly cooked or canned black beans
4 ripe plum tomatoes, diced
1/4 cup chopped cilantro leaves

If using fresh corn, preheat oven to 375 degrees F. Remove the tough outer husks and the corn silk. Place the ears directly on the oven rack and bake for 15 minutes. When cool enough to handle, husk the corn, cut the kernels from the cobs, and place the kernels in a medium-sized nonreactive bowl. Add the oil and garlic and mix to combine.

If using frozen corn, heat oil in a small skillet over high heat. Add the garlic and corn and cook, stirring, over high heat until the corn is browned. Transfer to a medium-sized nonreactive bowl and set aside to cool.

Add the remaining ingredients and mix to combine. Serve at room temperature; do not refrigerate.

FRIED GREEN PLANTAIN CHIPS

Festival de la Familia

Plaintains, which are commonly found in Latin American cooking, look like bananas. When green, they are considered a starch and can be prepared many ways. Here, they tastefully upstage the common potato chip.

Makes 1 1/2 quarts

2 green plantains, thinly sliced
Canola or corn oil, for frying
Salt to taste

Slice plantains on the bias paper-thin. Heat oil to 350 degrees F and fry chips in batches until crispy. Drain and sprinkle with salt. You can season with your favorite seasonings (garlic salt, cayenne, etc.).

GRILLED FLANK STEAK WITH MOJO MARINADE

Festival de la Familia

Cuban cuisine relies heavily on mojo, a citrus marinade accented with spices. To maximize the sweet and sour flavors of this outstanding mixture, allow the meat to marinate overnight.

Makes 4 servings

Mojo

10 cloves garlic
2 habaneros or other spicy chiles, cored, seeded, and minced (wear rubber gloves)
1 teaspoon kosher salt
1 teaspoon cumin
1 teaspoon paprika
1 cup olive oil
1/2 cup orange juice
1/2 cup lime juice
1/2 teaspoon crushed red pepper flakes
Salt and freshly ground black pepper to taste

Steak

1 1/2 pounds flank steak
Salt and freshly ground black pepper
2 large Bermuda onions, thickly sliced and brushed with olive oil

To make the mojo: In a food processor, add all ingredients and process until a paste forms. Scrape the mixture into a bowl and set aside.

For the steak: Put the steak in a resealable plastic bag or a shallow bowl and pour in 1 cup of the mojo. Seal and refrigerate for at least 2 hours or overnight, turning occasionally. Refrigerate the remaining 1 cup of mojo.

Preheat a grill to medium-high heat. Remove the steak from the marinade

(discard the marinade), pat dry, and season with salt and pepper; grill 5 to 7 minutes on one side and 3 to 4 minutes on the other for medium-rare. Remove from the grill and let rest for 5 minutes. While the steak is resting, grill the onions over medium-high heat until tender and slightly charred, 3 to 4 minutes per side.

Warm the reserved mojo over low heat. Slice the flank steak very thinly on the bias and serve with the reserved mojo and the grilled onions.

ARROZ CON POLLO (RICE WITH CHICKEN)

Festival de la Familia

This common Latin American dish uses saffron. Per pound, it is the most expensive spice in the world. The delicate threads are actually hand-picked flower stigmas and even the tiniest amount will impart an intense color and flavor to any dish.

Makes 8 servings

1/4 cup olive oil
2 whole chickens, about 3 pounds each, quartered
2 green bell peppers, chopped
1 large onion, chopped
5 cloves garlic, minced
1 (12-ounce) can tomatoes, chopped
8 saffron threads
4 cups chicken broth
2 bay leaves
2 whole cloves
Salt and freshly ground black pepper
2 cups rice
1 cup frozen peas
1 cup diced red bell pepper

In a stockpot over medium-high heat, heat oil and brown chicken on both sides. Add green pepper, onion, and garlic, and cook for about 5 minutes. Add tomato, saffron, broth, bay leaves, and cloves, and season with salt and pepper. Cover and cook for 20 minutes.

Add rice, stir well, cover again, and simmer for 20 to 30 minutes longer, or until all liquid has been absorbed and chicken is tender. Add peas and red pepper the last 5 minutes of cooking.

GUMBO
GUS'S
FRIED CHICKEN
NOW OPEN
SHADE TREE
NO SWIM'N

CORNCAKES WITH ROASTED RED PEPPER SAUCE

Great Southern Food Festival

If you're looking for a high-end, memorable pancake recipe, this is it. From the Wishbone Restaurant in Chicago, it contains all sorts of extras like corn, green onions, and a delicious red pepper sauce.

Makes about 32 corncakes

Corncakes

3/4 cup all-purpose flour
6 tablespoons yellow cornmeal
2 teaspoons sugar
1/4 teaspoon plus 1 pinch salt
1/4 teaspoon baking powder
1/4 teaspoon baking soda
2 1/4 cups buttermilk
2 eggs, separated
1 1/2 tablespoons Tabasco sauce
2 tablespoons unsalted butter, melted
1/4 cup cream-style corn
2/3 cup corn kernels, coarsely chopped
2 green onions, thinly sliced
1/4 cup fresh bread crumbs
1/4 cup vegetable oil

Sauce

1/2 cup white wine
3 shallots, minced
1/4 cup heavy cream
1/2 cup unsalted butter, cut into 8 pieces
2 red bell peppers, roasted, peeled, seeded, and puréed

To make the corncakes: Mix the flour, cornmeal, sugar, 1/4 teaspoon salt, baking powder, and baking soda.

In a bowl, whisk together the buttermilk, egg yolks, Tabasco sauce, and melted butter. With a wooden spoon, stir in the creamed corn, corn kernels, and green onions. Add the dry-ingredient mixture and stir just to blend. Add the bread crumbs and mix well. (This can be done the day before and refrigerated.)

Beat the egg whites with a pinch of salt to a stiff peak. Fold into the batter.

To make the sauce: Combine the wine and shallots in a saucepan and reduce by half over medium-high heat. Add the cream and cook until reduced by half. Lower the heat to medium-low and whisk in the butter, working on and off the stove, until it emulsifies. Add the peppers and keep the sauce warm over very low heat. If it separates, whisk it together.

Heat 1 tablespoon of the oil in a large nonstick skillet over medium-high heat. Pour in the batter to form corncakes 2 1/2 inches in diameter. Cook until bubbles form on the tops, 2 to 3 minutes. Flip the cakes and cook until they spring back when touched, 1 to 2 minutes. Repeat with the remaining batter, adding oil as necessary. Keep warm in a low oven or serve with some sauce poured over the cakes.

BEER BARBECUE SAUCE

Great Southern Food Festival

This versatile sauce can be used with just about any meat, fish, or poultry you would like to grill. It has the traditional sweet and sour flavors of most marinades with the beer for an extra kick.

Makes about 2 1/2 cups

1/2 cup chopped onions
1 tablespoon chopped garlic
1 tablespoon oil
2 (2-ounce) cans tomato paste
1 cup firmly packed brown sugar
1/3 cup Dijon mustard
1 teaspoon dry mustard
1 tablespoon soy sauce
1/4 cup Worcestershire sauce
1 tablespoon hot pepper sauce
1/4 cup vinegar
1 tablespoon lemon juice
1/2 teaspoon pepper
1 bottle beer

Sauté onions and garlic in oil. Add other ingredients. Simmer until well blended and allow to cool. Marinate meat (chicken, fish, steak, pork, ribs) overnight. Cook meat over hot grill, while basting with marinade.

CHOCOLATE PECAN CHOCOLATE CHUNK PIE

Great Southern Food Festival

It is no surprise that this luscious version of an American favorite came from *Cook-Off America's* co-host, Marcel Desaulniers. From his delightfully decadent cookbook, *Death by Chocolate Cakes* (William Morrow & Co., 2000), the "Guru of Ganache" notes that this dessert can be served chilled, at room temperature, or—for a really exquisite taste and texture—warmed.

Makes 12 servings

Tart Shell Dough
1 3/4 cups all-purpose flour
6 tablespoons unsalted butter, cut into 1-tablespoon pieces
1 tablespoon granulated sugar
Pinch of salt
1/4 cup ice water

Filling
1/2 cup (1 stick) unsalted butter
1/2 cup granulated sugar
12 ounces semisweet chocolate, chopped into 1/4-inch pieces
2 ounces unsweetened chocolate, chopped into 1/4-inch pieces
1 1/2 cups dark corn syrup
1 tablespoon pure vanilla extract
1/4 teaspoon salt
8 eggs
3 cups pecan halves

To make the tart shell: Mix 1 1/4 cups flour, butter, sugar, and salt in the bowl of an electric stand mixer fitted with a paddle. Mix on low speed for 5 minutes, until the butter is cut into the flour and has a mealy texture. Add the ice water and continue to mix on low for 10 to 15 seconds, until the dough comes together. Remove the dough from the mixer and form into a smooth round ball. Wrap in plastic wrap and refrigerate for at least 4 hours.

Remove the chilled dough from the refrigerator to a lightly floured work surface. Roll the dough (using the remaining 1/2 cup flour as needed to keep the dough from sticking) into a circle about 15 inches in diameter and 1/8 inch thick. Line a 9 by 1 1/2-inch springform pan with the dough, gently pressing it into the bottom and up the sides. Use a serrated knife to trim the excess dough, leaving a 3/4-inch border, which should be crimped around the top edge of the pan. Refrigerate the pie shell for 30 minutes.

To prepare the filling: Preheat the oven to 325 degrees F. Heat the butter and sugar in a 2 1/2 quart saucepan over medium-high heat, stirring constantly, bring the mixture to a boil, and boil for 1 1/2 minutes. Remove from the heat and transfer to the bowl of an electric stand mixer fitted with a paddle. Use a rubber spatula to stir in 6 ounces semisweet chocolate and the unsweetened chocolate. Continue to stir until the chocolate has melted. Add the corn syrup, vanilla extract, and salt. Add the eggs and combine on medium speed until the eggs are incorporated and the mixture is smooth. Remove the bowl from the mixer and finish combining the mixture with a rubber spatula.

Remove the pie shell from the refrigerator and place it on a baking sheet. Spread the pecans evenly over the bottom of the shell and top with the remaining 6 ounces semisweet chocolate. Slowly pour in the chocolate batter. Bake the pie on the baking sheet on the middle shelf of the oven for 1 hour. Lower the temperature to 300 degrees F and bake for an additional 45 to 55 minutes, until the internal temperature of the pie reaches 170 degrees F. remove from the oven and cool at room temperature for 1 hour. Refrigerate the pie in the pan for at least 2 hours.

To serve, cut the pie with a serrated knife, heating the blade under hot running water before making each slice. Serve immediately.

DEEP DISH PIZZA

Taste of Chicago

Chicago has a significant place in pizza history—the city immortalized the deep-dish variety that Ike Seawell created in 1943. Note this dough recipe has a rich crust with a combination of cornmeal and flour. As for the toppings, don't be a slave to any pizza recipe—use whatever and however much of it you like.

Makes one 14-inch pizza

Dough

1 package rapid-rise dry yeast
1 cup warm water
1/3 cup plus 1 teaspoon olive oil
3 1/2 cups flour
1/4 teaspoon salt
1/4 teaspoon black pepper

Pizza Topping (for a 14-inch pan)

2 tablespoons olive oil
1 (14 1/2-ounce) can chopped tomatoes in juice
Salt and pepper to taste
1 teaspoon chopped fresh basil
1 teaspoon chopped fresh oregano
1 teaspoon chopped fresh flat-leaf parsley
2 cloves garlic, minced
1/2 pound grated mozzarella cheese
3 tablespoons grated Parmesan cheese

To make the dough: In the bowl of an electric stand mixer, dissolve the yeast in the water. Add the olive oil, 2 cups of the flour, salt, and pepper. Beat with a paddle for 2 minutes. Attach the dough hook and mix in the remaining flour. Knead for 5 to 6 minutes with the mixer. (Note: Because the dough is very rich and moist, it would be difficult to do this by hand.)

Oil a 14-inch deep-dish pizza pan. Remove dough from the mixer bowl and place in the oiled pan. Cover with a very large metal bowl or towel and allow to rise until double in bulk, about 1 hour. Punch down the dough with your fingers and allow to rise again for about another hour. Punch down a second time, pushing the dough outward and being sure that the dough is all the way to the edge of the pan. You are now ready to make pizza!

To make the topping: Preheat the oven to 475 degrees F. Drizzle the oil over the dough. Sprinkle the diced tomatoes and juice over the pizza crust being sure to leave room at the edges for the crust (about 3/4 inch around the outer edge). Season the tomatoes with salt and pepper. Sprinkle on the basil, oregano, parsley, and garlic. Top the pizza with the two grated cheeses. Bake the pie on the center rack of the preheated oven until the top is golden and gooey and the crust a light golden brown, about 35 to 40 minutes.

Variations

You can add any or all of the following before you add the cheese:

Italian sausage
Pepperoni, thinly sliced
Mushrooms, thinly sliced
Olives
Bell peppers, cored and thinly sliced
Onions
Anchovies
Ham
Bacon

CHICKEN VESUVIO

Taste of Chicago

This dish is found in Italian restaurants throughout Chicago. The recipe makes a hearty chicken and potato braise cooked in an abundance of garlic and white wine. The dish has traditionally been served in the style inspired by its namesake, Mount Vesuvius—a mountain of potatoes are served around a crater of chicken. This version comes from *The Chicago Tribune Good Eating Cookbook* by Carol Mighton Haddix (McGraw-Hill, 2000).

Makes 4 servings

1/3 cup flour
1 1/2 teaspoons dried basil
3/4 teaspoon dried oregano
1/2 teaspoon salt
1/4 teaspoon dried thyme
1/4 teaspoon freshly ground black pepper
1/8 teaspoon dried rosemary
1/8 teaspoon rubbed sage
1 broiler/fryer chicken (about 3 pounds), cut into pieces
1/2 cup olive oil
3 baking potatoes, cut into lengthwise wedges
3 cloves garlic, minced
3 tablespoons minced fresh parsley
3/4 cup dry white wine

Mix flour, basil, oregano, salt, thyme, pepper, rosemary, and sage in a shallow dish. Dredge chicken in flour mixture. Shake off excess.

Heat oil in a 12-inch cast-iron or other ovenproof skillet over medium-high heat until hot. Add chicken pieces in a single layer. Fry, turning occasionally, until light brown on all sides, about 15 minutes. Remove and place on paper towels. Repeat until all pieces are fried.

Add the potato wedges to the same skillet. Fry, turning occasionally, until light brown on all sides, about 15 minutes. Remove and place on paper towels.

Preheat oven to 375 degrees F. Pour off all but 2 tablespoons of the fat from the skillet. Put the chicken and potatoes back in the skillet. Sprinkle with garlic and parsley. Pour wine over all.

Bake, uncovered, until potatoes are fork-tender, thigh juices run clear, and the internal temperature of the chicken reaches 170 degrees F, about 20 to 25 minutes. Let stand 5 minutes before serving. Serve with pan juices.

ELI'S STYLE ORIGINAL CHEESECAKE

Taste of Chicago

Here is another recipe from Carol Mighton Haddix's comprehensive *Chicago Tribune Good Eating Cookbook* (McGraw-Hill, 2000). Eli's cheesecake is a venerable Chicago institution that comes from the popular restaurant Eli's the Place for Steak. If you don't trust your cheesecake-making abilities or don't have time, check out www.elicheesecake.com where you can get it via mail order. Either way, you're in for a real treat.

Makes 12 servings

Crust

1 3/4 cups finely crushed vanilla wafers
6 tablespoons butter, melted

Filling

4 (8-ounce) packages cream cheese, softened
1 cup sugar
2 tablespoons all-purpose flour
2 large eggs
1 large egg yolk
6 tablespoons sour cream
1/2 teaspoon vanilla extract

To make the crust: Butter a 9-inch springform pan. In a small bowl, mix vanilla wafer crumbs with melted butter. Press crust into pan.

Preheat oven to 350 degrees F. Beat cream cheese, sugar, and flour in the bowl of an electric stand mixer until light and creamy, about 3 minutes. Add eggs and egg yolk one at a time, beating well after each addition. Add sour cream and vanilla. Beat, scraping down sides of the bowl, until smooth.

Pour mixture into prepared crust and place pan on a baking sheet. Bake till the cake edges are firm and the center barely jiggles when tapped, about 50 minutes. Refrigerate at least 8 hours. Top with your favorite fruit pie filling, sauce, or glaze.

FRIED ZUCCHINI STICKS

Hayward Zucchini Festival

These are a delicious treat and take just minutes to make. When deep-frying, make sure the oil is really hot or the food will absorb extra oil and become greasy. Japanese panko bread crumbs give the sticks an extra crunch, but regular bread crumbs can be substituted.

Makes 4 servings

1 cup flour
1 cup low-fat (2%) milk
2 cups panko crumbs
Salt and freshly ground black pepper to taste
2 zucchini, cut into 1/4 by 1/4-inch sticks
Vegetable oil

Place the flour, milk and panko crumbs in separate shallow bowls. Season flour and milk with salt and pepper. Bread zucchini sticks by dipping them first into the milk, then the seasoned flour, in the milk again, and finally in the panko crumbs.

Heat the vegetable oil in a large skillet over medium-high heat. Fry the zucchini until golden. Season with salt and pepper.

GRILLED ZUCCHINI AND BLACK EYE PEA SALAD

Hayward Zucchini Festival

In many areas of the South, black-eyed peas are served on New Year's Day because they are thought to bring good luck for the coming year. Of course, this is a great dish to serve any time of the year, especially with grilled main courses.

Makes 4 servings

2 zucchini, cut into 1/4-inch lengths
2 red onions, sliced 1/4 inch thick
3 teaspoons olive oil plus extra for brushing
Salt and freshly ground black pepper to taste
1 1/2 cups black-eyed peas
1 bunch green onions, cut on a bias
2 tomatoes, chopped into 1/4-inch pieces
3 teaspoons balsamic vinegar

Brush the zucchini and red onion with oil and season with salt and pepper. Grill the zucchini and red onion over medium heat until cooked through. Remove from the grill and allow to cool.

Dice the grilled vegetables and combine them in a medium bowl with the remaining ingredients. Gently toss. Taste and adjust the seasoning and serve at room temperature.

GRILLED STUFFED ZUCCHINI

Hayward Zucchini Festival

In true Italian style, zucchini is stuffed with a tasty combination of corn, red pepper, and red onion and topped with a coating of bread crumbs and Parmesan. They can be made a day ahead and cooked just before serving.

Makes 6 servings

3 zucchini, ends removed, cut in half lengthwise, and seeds removed
1 ear corn, husks and silk removed
2 tablespoons olive oil, plus extra for drizzling
Salt and freshly ground black pepper to taste
1 red pepper, roasted, skinned and seeded, and medium-diced
1 small red onion, finely diced
1/4 cup bread crumbs
1/2 cup shredded Parmesan cheese

Lightly brush the zucchini halves and the corn with 2 tablespoons of the oil. Season with salt and pepper and grill over medium-high heat until slightly charred and tender, about 3 minutes per side for the zucchini and about 10 minutes for the corn. Remove the zucchini and corn from the grill and allow to cool.

Use a sharp knife to remove the kernels from the corn cob and transfer them to a medium bowl. Add the roasted diced pepper and onion. Season with salt and pepper. Pack the cavities of the grilled zucchini with this vegetable mixture. Top the vegetable-stuffed zucchinis with the bread crumbs and Parmesan cheese. Drizzle oil over the tops and return to the upper rack of the grill to finish cooking for 2 minutes, until the onions are tender and the tops are golden brown. Remove from the grill and serve immediately.

MIMI MONTANO'S CHOCOLATE ZUCCHINI CAKE

Hayward Zucchini Festival

Real chocoholics know that any recipe from our host and master chocolatier, Marcel Desaulniers, is going to be over the top. This comes from his book *Death by Chocolate Cakes* (William Morrow & Co., 2000).

Makes 18 servings

1 tablespoon unsalted butter, melted
3 cups all-purpose flour
2 teaspoons ground cinnamon
1 1/2 teaspoons baking powder
1 teaspoon baking soda
1 teaspoon salt
1 large zucchini (about 3/4 pound), washed and stem removed
1 1/2 cups granulated sugar
4 large eggs
1 1/2 cups vegetable oil
3 ounces unsweetened baking chocolate, coarsely chopped and melted
1 (12-ounce) package semisweet chocolate chips (2 cups)

Preheat the oven to 325 degrees F. Liberally coat the inside of a 9 1/2 by 4-inch nonstick angel food cake pan with the melted butter. Set aside.

In a sifter, combine the flour, cinnamon, baking powder, baking soda, and salt. Sift onto a large piece of parchment paper (or waxed paper) and set aside until needed.

Grate the zucchini in a food processor fitted with a medium grating disk (or use a box grater). Set aside.

Place the sugar and eggs in the bowl of an electric stand mixer fitted with a paddle. Beat on medium-high speed for 2 minutes until light in color and thickened; then use a spatula to scrape down the sides of the bowl. Operate the mixer on medium while slowly adding the vegetable oil in a steady stream. (It's a good idea to use the

pouring shield attachment or cover the top of the mixer and sides of the bowl with a towel or plastic wrap to avoid splattering oil outside the bowl.) Continue to mix until the batter is yellow in color and thick, about 1½ minutes. Scrape down the sides of the bowl. Add the melted chocolate and mix for 30 seconds on medium speed. Continue to operate the mixer on medium and slowly add the sifted dry ingredients. Mix until incorporated, about 1 minute. Add the grated zucchini and mix on low for 15 seconds. Add the chocolate chips and mix on low another 15 seconds. Remove the bowl from the mixer and use a rubber spatula to finish mixing the batter until thoroughly combined. Transfer the batter to the prepared angel food cake pan, using a rubber spatula to spread it evenly.

Place the pan onto a baking sheet with sides on the center rack of the oven. Bake until a wooden skewer inserted in the center comes out clean, about 1 hour and 15 minutes. Remove the cake from the oven and cool in the pan for 30 minutes at room temperature. Unmold the cake from the pan. Place the cake, baked top facing up, on a cake circle (or onto a cake plate) and cool at room temperature for 1 more hour before slicing.

To serve, heat the blade of a serrated knife under hot running water and wipe the blade dry before cutting each slice. Serve immediately, or wrap in plastic wrap.

Little House Of eGGplaNt
PRODUCE

EGGPLANT AND ROASTED RED PEPPER WONTONS WITH CILANTRO PESTO

Loomis Eggplant Festival

The eggplant, red pepper, and goat cheese make a wonderful filling for this wonton, which goes together quickly. Thank you to Executive Chef David Hill from the Horseshoe Bar Grill in Loomis, California, for sharing this recipe.

Makes 24 wontons

Wontons

2 cups diced eggplant, skins removed
1 shallot, diced
2 cloves garlic, minced
1/4 cup olive oil
1/2 cup diced roasted red pepper, with no seeds or skins
3 ounces goat cheese
Salt and pepper to taste
1 egg
1/4 cup water
24 wonton wrappers
6 cups peanut oil

Cilantro Pesto

1/4 cup chopped cilantro
1/4 cup pine nuts
2 ounces Parmesan cheese
1 1/2 tablespoons minced garlic
2/3 cup olive oil
Salt and freshly ground black pepper to taste
Cilantro sprigs, for garnish

To make the wontons: In a skillet over medium-high heat, sauté the eggplant, shallots, and garlic in olive oil until the eggplant is soft. Allow to cool. In a bowl, mix eggplant mixture, roasted red peppers, goat cheese, salt, and pepper until well combined.

Mix egg and water. Coat edges of each wonton wrapper with egg mixture to help seal. Fill each wonton with 1 tablespoon filling and seal by bringing the top to the center. Refrigerate for 1 hour. Heat the peanut oil in a heavy saucepot to 375 degrees F. Remove the wontons from the refrigerator and fry until golden brown; drain.

To make the pesto: Mix all ingredients in a food processor until smooth. Serve on the side of the wontons arranged on a small plate. Garnish with sprigs of cilantro.

EGGPLANT BRUSCHETTA

Loomis Eggplant Festival

While most people think of bruschetta as an hors d'oeuvre, this makes a lovely and attractive first course. The dish can be prepared ahead of time up to the last step and then placed in the oven just prior to serving. This is one of several winning recipes included in the *Loomis Eggplant Festival Cookbook.*

Makes 8 servings

8 (3/4-inch-thick) slices herb bread
1/3 cup olive oil
1 eggplant
Salt to taste
8 slices mozzarella cheese
1/4 cup chopped fresh basil
2 tomatoes, sliced
3 or 4 slices red onion
1/2 cup crumbled Gorgonzola cheese
2 tablespoons balsamic vinegar

Preheat oven to 400 degrees F.

Brush slices of bread with olive oil and place on a baking sheet. Slice the eggplant in 1/4-inch slices and place on the baking sheet as well. Bake for 10 minutes or until lightly browned. Remove from the oven and lightly salt the eggplant slices. On toasted bread slices, place mozzarella, baked eggplant, basil, tomato slices, onion, and Gorgonzola.

Drizzle balsamic vinegar over bruschetta. Return to the oven and bake until cheese is thoroughly melted, about 7 or 8 minutes.

ROASTED EGGPLANT AND RED PEPPER DIP

Loomis Eggplant Festival

Another festival winner by Martha Merriam and Sarah McGlinn, this dip is a wonderful blend of different flavors and well worth the effort involved. Try grilling the eggplant, bell pepper, and garlic for extra flavor.

Makes about 3 cups

2 medium or 1 large eggplant, cut in half (will make 2 cups roasted)
1 head garlic, with top sliced off
1 large bell pepper (will make 1 cup roasted)
1/2 cup walnuts
3/4 teaspoon cumin
1/2 cup bread crumbs
6 teaspoons pomegranate jelly
3/4 teaspoon chili powder
1 tablespoon toasted almond oil
1/2 teaspoon salt
Juice of 1 lemon

Roast eggplant and garlic in a 375 degree F oven for 1 hour. Turn oven to broil.

Line a broiler pan with foil and place the pepper in it. Turning occasionally, broil the pepper close to heat for 10 minutes, until charred or blistered. Wrap foil around the pepper to steam it at room temperature for 15 minutes.

Lower oven heat to 350 degrees F. Spread walnuts on a baking sheet and bake 8 to 10 minutes until toasted. In a saucepan, toast cumin over low heat until fragrant. Remove pepper from foil. Peel off skin, discard seeds, and cut pepper into large pieces. Scrape the soft eggplant out into a measuring cup. Peel the outer skin from the garlic head and release the roasted garlic cloves (8 to 10 cloves are needed).

In food processor grind the walnuts until ground. Add the bread crumbs and blend. Add eggplant, peppers, garlic, and the remaining ingredients. Blend until smooth. Transfer to bowl. Cover and refrigerate if not serving right away.

ANDALUSIAN GAZPACHO SALAD

TomatoFest

Gazpacho originated in Spain, where the hot days dictated a cool treat. Tomatoes are the star of this chunky version, which eats like a delicious summer salad.

Makes 8 servings

2 garlic cloves, peeled
3 tablespoons freshly squeezed lemon juice
4 tablespoons Solera sherry
1 teaspoon sugar
Salt to taste
2 tablespoons extra virgin olive oil
2 pounds ripe red and yellow heirloom tomatoes, seeded and diced
1 pound cucumbers, peeled and diced
2 red bell peppers, diced
1 red onion, finely chopped
1/2 cup chopped fresh mint and cilantro
Freshly ground black pepper to taste
1/2 cup goat cheese, crumbled

Rub a large wooden bowl with garlic; mash garlic and leave in bowl. Add lemon juice, sherry, sugar, salt, and olive oil; blend mixture with a whisk. Add remaining ingredients except goat cheese and toss. Add goat cheese; season with salt and pepper. Refrigerate for at least 2 hours to let the flavors marry. Serve this with chicken or fish, or just serve it with your favorite chips. It is not a bad idea to just eat it with a spoon!

BABELE DI POMODORI (TOMATO TOWER)

TomatoFest

This striking recipe pays homage to the tomato in its simplest form. Sliced and combined with a myriad of ingredients, the tomato tower is as flavorful as it is beautiful.

Makes 4 servings

1 red tomato
1 yellow tomato
1 tiger tomato
1 slice smoked mozzarella cheese
2 slices fresh mozzarella cheese
4 fresh basil leaves
2 tablespoons fresh ricotta cheese
1 tablespoon chopped sundried tomato
3 pitted kalamata olives, chopped
1 bunch enoki mushrooms
4 fresh chive stems
3 leaves frisée lettuce
1 tablespoon lemon juice
3 tablespoons extra virgin olive oil
Salt and freshly ground black pepper to taste

Slice tomatoes $1/2$ inch thick. Using 5 pieces of the center slices, pile the first slice with smoked mozzarella; the second slice with fresh mozzarella, 2 basil leaves, and a pinch of salt; the third slice with 1 tablespoon ricotta and $1\frac{1}{2}$ teaspoons sundried tomato; the fourth slice with a mixture of the remaining ricotta, sundried tomatoes, basil leaves (chopped), and olives; top with the fifth slice of tomato.

With a paring knife, punch a hole on top of the tower and insert enoki mushrooms and chives. On a 9-inch plate, arrange frisée leaves and place the tower in the middle. Mix lemon juice, olive oil, salt, and pepper and drizzle this dressing over the tower.

TOMATO BRUNCH SANDWICH

TomatoFest

This brunch dish has wonderful layers of flavor and texture with its crunchy coating covering warmed tomatoes and herbed cream cheese. Be sure to use vine-ripened tomatoes, large enough to get three 1/2-inch slices from the center of each tomato.

Makes about 6 servings

4 large round red tomatoes (slightly firm)
8 ounces cream cheese, softened
1 clove garlic, crushed
1/4 cup parsley, minced
1 teaspoon fresh or 1/2 teaspoon dried basil
1/8 teaspoon salt
1/2 cup flour
1 egg, beaten with 1 tablespoon milk
2/3 cup seasoned bread crumbs
3 tablespoons butter
3 tablespoons olive oil

Slice tomatoes into 12 half-inch slices (do not use ends). In a medium bowl, mix together the cream cheese, garlic, parsley, basil, and salt. Spread about 2 tablespoons of this cream cheese filling on a tomato slice; place a second slice on top creating a "sandwich." Bread each "sandwich" by placing them in flour, then in the egg wash, and finally in seasoned bread crumbs.

In a skillet, melt the butter and heat the oil together and panfry the sandwiches on a low to medium fire till golden brown, approximately 5 to 10 minutes. Serve immediately.

VEGETABLE-STUFFED TOMATOES WITH WHITE BEAN VINAIGRETTE

TomatoFest

These superb baked and stuffed tomatoes come from *The Great Tomato Book* by Gary Ibsen (Ten Speed Press, 1999), and can be served at room temperature or chilled. They are filled with squash, artichokes, pepper, and cheese.

Makes 8 servings

White Bean Vinaigrette

1 1/4 cups Great Northern (white) beans, soaked in water overnight
2 cups chicken stock or water
1 small carrot, chopped in 2 or 3 pieces
1 small onion, halved
3 sprigs thyme
1 1/2 cups red cherry tomatoes
4 shallots, finely chopped
1/4 cup sherry wine vinegar
3/4 cup extra virgin olive oil
1/4 cup chopped fresh parsley
1/4 cup chopped fresh basil
Salt and freshly ground black pepper to taste

Vegetable-Stuffed Tomatoes

3 tablespoons extra virgin olive oil
1 red onion, chopped
1 1/2 cups chopped summer squash, such as zucchini, sunburst, or patty pan
3 tablespoons lemon marmalade
1 1/2 cups chopped cooked artichoke hearts
1 large sweet Hungarian pepper, roasted, peeled, seeded, and chopped (about 1/2 cup)
8 ounces goat cheese, crumbled
1 tablespoon fresh thyme leaves

1/4 cup coarsely chopped basil
Salt and freshly ground black pepper to taste
8 tomatoes, preferably bell pepper tomatoes or stuffer tomatoes, which are hollow inside
1 cup fresh bread crumbs

Simmer the beans, chicken stock, carrots, onions, and thyme in a medium saucepan for about 1 1/2 hours, or until the beans are tender. (Add more liquid if the beans are not completely covered while cooking.) Drain the beans, reserving 1/4 cup of the liquid, and discard the thyme sprigs, carrot, and onion. Allow the beans to cool.

Place the beans in a medium bowl and add the reserved bean liquid, the cherry tomatoes, shallots, vinegar, olive oil, parsley, and basil. Season with salt and pepper.

To prepare the tomatoes: Heat 1 tablespoon of the olive oil in a medium sauté pan over medium-low heat. Add the onion and sauté for 3 to 5 minutes, or until transparent. Add the squash and lemon marmalade and sauté for 2 to 3 minutes, or until the squash is still crispy tender. Remove from the heat and add the artichoke hearts, sweet pepper, goat cheese, thyme, and basil. Mix well and season with salt and black pepper.

Preheat the oven to 400 degrees F. Slice the tops off the tomatoes. Slice about 1/8 inch off the bottoms of tomatoes, so they stand upright. If not using stuffer-type tomatoes, hollow out firm red tomatoes and discard excess pulp and seeds. Stuff with the vegetable mixture. Sprinkle with the bread crumbs and drizzle with the remaining 2 tablespoons of olive oil. Bake for 15 minutes. Set aside to cool. When ready to serve, place the stuffed tomatoes on a platter or on individual plates and surround them with the White Bean Vinaigrette.

COOK-OFF AMERICA KITCHEN COURTESY OF WOOD-MODE

ABOUT OUR HOSTS

Marcel Desaulniers

After attending the Culinary Institute of America, Marcel worked in private New York City clubs with European chefs and then at Colonial Williamsburg, Virginia. To refine his skills, he took and taught cooking classes in Europe and the United Sates.

In 1980 Marcel and partner John Curtis opened The Trellis. The restaurant's success led Marcel to publish his first book, *The Trellis Cookbook,* in 1988.

As the first Southern chef to be named by the James Beard Foundation as a Great American Chef and the recipient of many other awards, Marcel has taken his place among the country's culinary elite.

Carolyn O'Neil

Carolyn is a registered dietician and an award-winning journalist with over 20 years' experience in nutrition and cuisine.

After joining CNN in 1982, she developed the network's food beat, served as executive producer and senior correspondent for CNN's highly rated *On the Menu,* and anchored *CNN Travel Now.*

Winner of two James Beard Awards for television food journalism and accolades from the National Restaurant Association, the American Heart Association, and the American Dietetic Association, she was chosen TV Personality Woman of Achievement in Atlanta. In 1999, she was named Best TV Food Journalist during the World Cookbook Fair in France.

ACKNOWLEDGMENTS

The Cook-Off America television series and this companion cookbook would not have been possible without the tremendous support and talented efforts of a very special group of people and companies.

We are extremely privileged to work with two tremendously talented hosts, **Marcel Desaulniers** and **Carolyn O'Neil,** whose performances and professionalism throughout the making of the programs were truly inspiring. Despite the grueling hours and rigors of production, they brought both wisdom and expertise to the set along with endless enthusiasm.

We are honored to have the continuing support of the **Weber-Stephen Products Company** and especially **Mike Kempster, Sr.,** whose unwavering enthusiasm and invaluable advice have played such a key role in *Cook-Off America*'s success. As we travel all over the country filming food festivals, we continually see how the Weber grills have become a symbol of great barbecue and such an important part of the outdoor cooking experience.

We would also like to extend a big thank-you to the supportive staff at **Cascade** and **Procter & Gamble,** especially **Kristen Nostrand** and **Lela Coffey**. We are proud to be associated with a company so committed to providing quality household products to homes around the country. It is no surprise that Cascade products have become an essential part of so many kitchens.

A heartfelt thanks goes out to **Bill Tobin** and **Wood-Mode,** the creators of our beautiful television set, which is just one striking example of the superior quality and unrivaled craftsmanship found in their fine cabinetry. Of course, kitchens need more than cabinets to create great food, and—thanks to the ever-gracious **Brian Maynard**—we were delighted to have use of the outstanding line of KitchenAid appliances for all the mixing, shredding, dicing, slicing—and washing—we needed to do. As usual, the **KitchenAid** appliances stood up beautifully to some highly intense usage and always created perfect results.

We are very grateful to **Reynolds Wrap,** whose products have been an indispensable ingredient both on and off the set. Reynolds products consistently reflect innovation and ingenuity with the home cook in mind.

We'd also like to extend our gratitude to the **Singapore Tourism Board** who did so much to help us in the filming of the Singapore Food Festival. Their guidance and support was invaluable and allowed us to see a side to Singapore we might have overlooked. A big thank-you also to the **Big Island Visitors Bureau** and their PR firm, **Current Events,** for their help and support in our filming of the Kona Coffee Cultural Festival. We are very grateful to the **National**

Watermelon Promotion Board for pointing the way to Luling, Texas, a place every watermelon lover should visit. We also received tremendous support from the **Jamaica Tourist Board,** who made it possible for us to film the spectacular Jamaica Spice Festival, and the **Mendocino County Alliance** for their assistance with our filming of Mendocino Crab and Wine Days. And another big thank-you to our friends at **Johnson & Wales University,** especially **Jim Lyle** and **Brenda Bassett,** who sponsor the exciting Bacardi Recipe Classic and who made it possible for us to include it in our series.

There are never enough thanks that we can bestow upon our kitchen supervisor, **Brett Bailey,** with his boundless energy and unrelenting pursuit of perfection in the kitchen. Along with the steadfast support of chef **Jason Wade,** he researched, prepped, and prepared each recipe to flawless precision.

Big accolades go to our associate producer, **Deanna Sison.** As a result of her excellent research, we had a remarkable group of festivals and recipes to include in the series and book. She handled an indeterminate number of logistical elements for the project in her customary competent, efficient, and unflappable way.

We'd also like to acknowledge the staff of MJA Studios in Vancouver, especially **Wolf Isachsen** and **Adam Buonsanti,** who provided such excellent studio accommodations. Finally, a huge thank-you to our wonderful technical director, **Michael Varga,** whose unrelenting and meticulous attention to the technical side of production always produces first-rate results.

Marjorie Poore
Alec Fatalevich
Producers

INDEX

190